D1564772

EYES SHUT

FEDERIGO

TOZZI

EYES SHUT

A Novel

Translated by Kenneth Cox

CARCANET

First published in English in 1990 by
Carcanet Press Limited
208–212 Corn Exchange Buildings
Manchester M4 3BQ

Translated from *Con gli occhi chiusi*,
published by Treves in Milan, 1919.
Translation copyright © Kenneth Cox 1990

British Library Cataloguing in Publication Data

Tozzi, Federigo, *1883-1920*
   Eyes shut.
   I. Title   II. [Con gli occhi chiusi. *English*]
   853′.912[F]

   ISBN 0-85635-809-6

The publisher acknowledges financial assistance
from the Arts Council of Great Britain

Typeset in 11/13pt Bembo by Paragon Photoset, Aylesbury
Printed and bound in England by SRP Ltd, Exeter

Foreword

The life and work of the Italian writer Federigo Tozzi are as yet little known in English-speaking countries. He tells the story of his childhood and youth in the following novel, called in the original *Con gli occhi chiusi*. It is only necessary to add a few particulars and note what happened after.

Tozzi was born in Siena on New Year's Day 1883. His book, describing his life with his bully of a father and his infatuation with a young country girl, takes him up to the age of about twenty, most of it covering the years round the turn of the century. Some facts are altered (his mother died a few years before he says she did and his father did remarry though he says he did not) but the substance is true, in places brutally frank. The outstanding features are honest recording of painful experience and sharp pictures of the surrounding life, with some things he cannot have known vividly imagined. It was written, after his father's death and his marriage to a doctor's daughter, in 1913 but not published until 1919. Previously he had brought out two books of juvenile verse, one of prose sketches and three anthologies of writing by the medieval Sienese.

Soon after the novel was published Tozzi fell ill and on 21 March 1920 he died of pneumonia. The little notice his book received was mainly unfavourable but another novel written recently, *Tre croci*, a story about three brothers

5

who kept a bookshop in Siena, was already in the press and this was more successful: an English translation (*Three crosses*) appeared in 1921. But much that Tozzi had written remained in manuscript or buried in little magazines. His widow and later his son have most of the credit for bringing it to light. Three other novels, all autobiographical in origin, appeared at intervals and eventually a collected edition was brought out. This gave Tozzi's work a place in Italian literature but his standing with readers remained low, chiefly because of changes of interest and errors of judgement. There were also difficulties with his language and his distinctive way of writing.

Tozzi does not so much flout the conventions of fiction as seem unaware that any exist. In an answer to hostile reviewers he declared he had invented his technique himself and owed nothing to foreigners. He had however studied the medieval Sienese writings and in addition had a pictorial model. He had wanted to be a painter and many of the characteristics of his work look like attempts to do in language what a painter would do in paint. The clarity and intensity of his writing, its concentration on fugitive states each rendered in autonomous detail, are indebted to medieval Sienese art.

The rediscovery of Tozzi began in the mid-1960s, when the literary critic Giacomo Debenedetti made *Con gli occhi chiusi* the starting-point of his reappraisal of modern Italian fiction and the novelist Carlo Cassola pronounced it 'the most original novel in our literature'. Today almost all Tozzi's prose is collected in one thin-paper volume and his principal novels are available in paperback. *Con gli occhi chiusi* was not however translated into any language until 1971, when it came out in Czech. Seventy years after its original publication it appears in English.

K.C.

6

Eyes Shut

THE WAITERS and the kitchen staff had gone, leaving Domenico Rosi, the owner of the restaurant, to tot up the takings by the light of a guttering candle. Coming upon two fifty-lira notes his fingers closed and before tucking the notes into his wallet of chrome-tanned calf he had another look at them folded together. Then, bringing his mouth beside the puny flame, he blew. If the candle hadn't swealed away he'd have counted the money in the other till as well, his wife's, but he pulled the street-door to and turned the key, kneeing hard to make sure it had locked. He lived across the road, almost opposite.

Thirty years this had been his routine but he could still recall the first money he'd worked for and every closing-time the recollection soothed him to the bottom of his soul. It was like a good day's take.

A restaurant of his own! At times, talking about it, he'd pat its walls with the flat of his hands, in boast and satisfaction.

Brought up in the country he'd quit farm-work early but was still countrified, ready with his fists if anybody didn't take him at his word. God he believed had co-partnered him in his success, as a sort of sop. Anyhow he felt a need to go on making money, it was a protection against ill-wishers. Plenty of people would do anything to see him back where he'd started, when he didn't have a bean!

Four sisters and three brothers were left in poverty at Civitella, a maremma village ringed by scrub thick with

9

wild boar, in their house of chipped stone with stairs wobbly to tread on, made of rocks from the river, and windows looking onto a mound of marl so near and so steep it seemed to be after them and might any day topple over. Rosi thought of the poky hole he'd grown up in as something that didn't exist any more, or only for others. Childhood memories meant as little to him as scenes on the stage or pictures in the paper, things he despised and detested. Fiddle-faddle, all very well for layabouts with money to burn. Like smoking. No one could say they'd ever seen him at the opera or, worse still, puffing a cigar. Catch him! Too fly for that!

No sooner was he settled in Siena, at twenty, than he married Anna, illegitimate so no dowry but quite good-looking and younger than himself, and opened an eating-house that in the course of time became one of the best restaurants in town: *The Blue Fish*.

Now they had one child, a boy coming up for thirteen called Pietro. But before him there'd been seven others who'd died one after the other almost as soon as they were taken from the wet-nurse. Out of concern for his health they'd delayed putting Pietro to school and then sent him to a seminary, this being nearest, as one of the day-boys who had lessons with the seminarists but came home afterwards and didn't have to dress like them. Her previous confinement had left Anna with convulsions. She'd always been liable to symptoms of hysteria, an illness that made Domenico laugh, a sort of joke he didn't understand. When the laughing did no good he got huffed, wounded in his pride. And there was the bill to pay at the chemist's.

After many years of marriage the docile and devoted Anna came to realize he was unfaithful. Several times she had a sensation her heart was being dragged down in a two-handed wrench. She felt she was growing old and ugly before her time. At the thought her eyes filled with tears but she never mentioned it: though kind to everyone she didn't want to have friends. But she felt choked, her charitable nature was outraged and as she inhaled her aromatic vinegar the tears trickled down to her lips.

Being chubby in the face, the way women are who've put on fat, her sudden flare-ups were misunderstood. Harmless in themselves they revealed a nervous disposition, resembling reflexes of animals in pain. It's true, people laugh if a hen with its throat cut goes into a flurry or a rabbit screams and tears its nails out!

Set on having an heir both she and Domenico came to regard the children who'd died as so many abstract attempts they'd been obliged to abandon: no doubt it was all for the best, if such was fate's will. So her love for Pietro was affection tinged with superstition. Temperamentally incapable of showing him much tenderness she always liked to have him near her. When he fell asleep on her shoulder she could never bring herself to let him be put to bed by Rebecca, who'd been his wet-nurse and now helped with the house-work and in the wine-cellar.

But Domenico, bustling about the kitchen, would call out without stopping his work:

– Carrying that lump yourself?

And in case he'd come and take the child up in those raw red arms of his, she'd wake him and bundle him off to bed. Next evening, vexed with herself for giving in, she'd whisper:

– You're a nuisance. Keep away from me.

Pietro took no notice but squeezed in between her and the arm-rest of her easy-chair, clinging to her hand and closing his eyes with sleep. Anna disengaged herself, as she had to give change to the waiters and shake hands with the customers coming and going. The restaurant continued filling up till late at night. Being busy stimulated her as well as the others but by midnight they were all ready to drop. If there was anybody still at table they dowsed the lights in the other rooms one by one. The waiters took off their jackets, the cooks changed out of their whites. Anna made use of these breathing-spaces to

11

finish her mending and also do a little embroidery, but quite plain, to keep down the cost and fancy work being beyond her. As a girl she'd been a housemaid and hadn't had time to learn anything. But she knew how to write and got so much practice adding up customers' bills never made a mistake.

She had everything kept neat and tidy: plates and bowls stacked on the top of an old meal-chest, loaves and wine-flasks stored in the pantry. And she could handle tradesmen. Lemons she selected herself, though under Domenico's eye and subject to his approval, with a finickiness that gave pleasure and made her feel proud. If the seller managed to fob her off with one lumpy or bruised, Domenico made him replace it, thrusting it under his nose.

Anna usually went to bed, if she could, an hour or so before he did. One night, when a drunken engine-driver wouldn't leave, Domenico lifted him bodily off his chair and carried him into the street. The driver flicked his knife and flew at him. Domenico dodged and the waiters interposed. Anna, who was there with her head wrapped in a woollen shawl such as she always had on, got such a shock her convulsions became more severe and more frequent. The doctor advised her to stay as much as she could at Poggio a' Meli, a smallholding Domenico had recently bought. Saturdays she came back, she couldn't be away from the restaurant on market-day. Pietro and Rebecca went with her. Domenico spent the night in Siena but every evening took his wife a hamper of food for the following day, in his gig, clamping it between his legs so it shouldn't fall off.

Poggio a' Meli lay outside the Porta Camollia on the rather lonely road that runs from the Palazzo dei Diavoli to a little past the monastery of Poggio al Vento. It had a small old single-storeyed dwelling-house distempered red, with vat-house attached and quarters for the labourers over the stalls for the beasts. Domenico thought the red jolly but Anna would have preferred, as one or two acquaintances had suggested, either a light blue or a canary yellow.

Just by the entry was the threshing-floor and on one side of it the well and a circular pleached arbour where in summer Domenico kept a dozen lemon-trees in tubs: his one luxury, there being no garden. These were his pride and joy, though the return on his outlay was small. Often, depending on the mood he was in, Pietro wasn't allowed to touch them even.

The holding was a few hectares hedged from the road with buckthorn and hawthorn. A tiny piece of arable, level and well tilled, the rest of the land shelving away to a foss at the foot of a low rise under the walls of the Porta Camollia.

The boundary was planted with stout black scrub-oaks, here and there a walnut- tree towering above them. Down in the bottom, where it was wet, osier willows and a vegetable patch. From the threshing-floor you could see Siena.

The last Sunday of the month, after mass, the labourers trooped to the restaurant and Domenico paid them their wages, making each scrawl a cross over the receipt stamps. It was then he explained what he wanted doing and discussed the work done. He always found fault, never omitting a threat to sack them. Then, repeating louder and louder the instructions they had to carry out the next day, he told them they could go home. And at once rolled his sleeves up and went into the kitchen, as now was the time customers came for lunch. Usually he had his own during the pay-out.

Small as it was and with the outbuildings arranged as they were, the farm was a pretty place with an inviting charm: five cypresses in a line behind the dwarf wall of the threshing-floor, then all close-set with olives and fruit. Some one looking round had said once: *If it was bigger it wouldn't be so nice.* The level tillage was a dark red-brown loam, the rest a dry hard tufa, almost yellow.

13

In spring wherever it hadn't been ploughed or dug it went a hundred shades of green that autumn took a while to turn.

The usual passers-by, varying with the time of day, were one or two monks in the mornings, farmers and their waggons all day long, and about noon every Thursday beggars making their way to the monastery for soup. In autumn there were also families staying at their villas and visitors at a guest-house. These spent the evenings out of doors. Sundays, if it was fine, parties having a singsong after drinking in the taverns and restaurants on the city's outskirts.

Leaving Siena the road is flat and narrow nearly all the way: several villas, more farms, then ilex, oak, chestnut, timber gates, clipped hedges, with a view of the much grander villas towards Marciano church and the hills heaped up in the direction of the maremma and Monte Amiata.

Whenever a farm changes hands and the new owner's no fool it soon begins to look different in a way people who know about farming see first and then everybody else does. And Domenico transformed Poggio a' Meli. He pulled up when blossom from peach and almond saplings he'd had planted blew into the middle of the road. Cursing, he cocked his eye up at the branches, now bare of all but leaves, and lashed out with his whip at Spot, who was barking and frisking about for excitement at his arrival. For hours he plodded along the vine-rows, peering for signs of the phylloxera. One of the men followed and always had to assure him it wasn't their fault. If a vine looked badly tied or a stake unsteady, he had another withy fetched and the job done again, there and then, under his eyes.

About pruning the olive-trees there were endless discussions. He stood the ladder where he judged best but didn't climb it himself because of his weight. From the ground below he told them which branches to cut out.

14

Or he taught them how to hold a spade so as to make it go in deeper.

When the wine was drawn off he scoured and rinsed the casks and tuns all by himself, never moving from the vat-tap.

As Anna had grown fond of Rebecca, jilted though pregnant, and Domenico liked her too, they'd added her old parents Giacco and Masa to the Poggio a' Meli labourers. They were poor and their other daughters had gone and got married so a few years later they approached the master with the request would he take on Ghisola too, a granddaughter of theirs born to one of Rebecca's sisters at Radda.

Giacco and Masa wouldn't have thrown a rusty old nail away. Giacco's green fustian trousers had so many patches only a few strips here and there were left of the original stuff. The headscarf Masa wore she'd bought when young.

She could never get meals ready on time and Giacco would lose patience and swear at her, watching every move she made. This confused her and made her take longer still. It was a sight to see! She let oil out of a little metal can in a needle-thin drip. When the lip had stopped dripping she licked it and licked it before locking the can in the meal-chest again. The pan boiled and she tossed in garlic and chopped onion. When the garlic turned yellowy-brown she tipped the fry into the stockpot filled with salted water. She set this on the fire again and meanwhile sliced a loaf, resting it on her chest and pressing the knife with both hands. Spot polished off the crumbs as they fell. Masa kicked him away, frantic: she'd been going to save them for the hens!

As soon as he came in Giacco had a wash in a copper basin all dents and took his seat, rubbing his stubby calloused fingers over his face.

Finally Masa poured the liquid over the slices of bread and Ghisola brought the twists of salt and pepper, getting

15

told off for scraping her back against the wall as she moved from one part of the room to another.

Giacco thought how the calf had snuffled his spine while he was filling its manger with grass, so that he'd pushed it away, saying: *You're getting me all smothered in hairs.* He ordered his wife:

– Put on the mash for the calf before you come and sit down. You know but you always pretend to forget.

When his work was done he had great tenderness for those nuzzlings in the byre, the calf's breath as warm and wet as his own sweat, and he ate without speaking, going over them in his mind.

Sometimes Anna knocked at their outer door. Then all three of them stood up.

– It's the mistress. Go and let her in. Look sharp!

A whole winter went by till Pietro saw Poggio a' Meli again. He only overheard his father talking to customers about it: new vines, a nursery of fruit-trees, heavier grain crops and the first grape harvest, the wine as clear as clear but tasting of sulphur and scalding the stomach.

Sometimes at the restaurant he came across Ghisola sitting in silence with her aunt Rebecca. He looked at her but made no approach. He didn't like her so much and it didn't seem they'd ever spoken.

After a few bouts of fever at the end of May he went to the farm with his mother again. The house being shut up several months in the year they always found it smelling of mice and plaster and the locks were stiff. They called Giacco, the first time, so as not to hurt their hands, and Masa was given the job of dusting the rooms and clearing away the cobwebs.

16

Ghisola helped too but she was not to touch anything that might break.

On his first day there Pietro had a bilious attack that made him pass out. The glands behind his ears ached, still swollen.

He tore up by the root any plant within reach, stripped shoots off the vines, struck at a tree with a stake till the bark peeled off. He pulled the legs and wings off grasshoppers and then skewered the bodies on a pin. He watched when a cloud was overhead and when it moved on waited for another one, as though to exhibit himself.

At last it rained, no thunder but a continuous spattering under the gutter-spouts. When the clouds thinned some splotches of sunlight lingered on the hills the other side of the rain, it screened them with threads so fine a gust could snap the lot. The rainbow appeared, as though it had been waiting to.

After supper Anna called Masa and the other labourers' wives into the farmhouse. They came in stumbling over each other at every step.

– Sit yourselves down.

They answered, as they always did:

– But we'll be in the way, ma'am.

– Sit down, I tell you.

Anna liked being mistress and having respect shown her but she was fond of them really.

Ghisola sat right at the back, watchful and serious. Pietro, supposed to be doing some school-work, took a look at the parting of her hair, drawn tight as cotton round a reel, then ignored her till his mother sent her to fetch a ball of wool from the next room. She obeyed rapidly, like a lifesize puppet, afterwards crouching in her corner again, eyes fixed on Anna's crochet-work, feet hooked on the strut of her chair.

Anna noticed and drew back slightly on the sofa. She lifted her hands and said:

– Now watch. You hold the hook like this, then take up

. . . loop round this way . . . and take up again. You can't go wrong.

Orsola, who had a strawberry nose, answered without having understood:

– Aren't you clever!

Masa turned to her granddaughter:

– Wouldn't you like to learn?

Then Orsola, scratching her head with a knitting needle, said:

– Ghisola's young, her fingers are limber. We can't twiddle ours like that.

– And we can't see so well either.

Adele added that, her eyesight was the weakest.

– We don't know how to do anything except boil a drop of water for our men. Even that we don't do properly.

They all laughed and Masa exclaimed:

– But look what delicate fingers the mistress has! It doesn't seem possible!

Anna set her work down and, blushing, laid her hand on the table, in the light, showing it this way and that. It was small and pudgy with swollen fingertips and stubbed nails.

Pietro was listening but they all seemed to be acting like figures in a dream and when his mother addressed him she had to repeat herself two or three times.

– What are you mooning over? You understand what we say.

A peculiar uneasiness made him afraid to answer. He left his chair to sit on the sofa, in the grip of a kind of dread he'd got used to, spellbound by a sense of remoteness that at times induced a terrifying bliss. Finally his head dropped to his knees with drowsiness. At a signal from Anna, Ghisola approached and just pinked his hand with a knitting needle, hardly touching him, to make him stir. At first he pretended he didn't feel it, to be still sunk in that caved-in chasm of his. Then, without raising his eyes, he was rude to her. Ghisola was now

18

part of the spiky reality that meant less to him than his states of withdrawal. He felt the difference with a sharp pang:

– You hurt me!

Not so calm now, his face was pale and drawn. Anna dismissed the girl earlier than usual so she shouldn't start crying. Ghisola had slunk away at once, timidly and as though slighted.

Rain had begun to fall again after sunset. It made a soft patter among the fireflies, as numerous as before. Some clung to corn-stalks, motionless and continuing to glow without flicker beneath the battering of the raindrops.

Pietro's eyes wouldn't stay open and dreamily he let his mother undress him. When he was in bed she gave him a glance and said:

– That's three nights you haven't said an Ave Maria. Bless yourself.

He would have done if he'd been more awake. He moved his arm but didn't get it as far as his forehead, feeling the sign of the cross being made over him and relishing what he'd said to Ghisola. He dozed off watching his mother circle the bed, shadow-like, to give him her blessing.

– You might at least say goodnight.

But he was sound asleep when Anna went, shielding him from the light of the candle with her body and having first placed his socks and pants under the eiderdown.

In the middle of the night he woke up. He could hear a nightingale, perhaps from the oaks by the threshing-floor. Its singing sounded like speech answered by a distant mate. He lay a long time listening to the pair, wishing he wasn't and thinking Ghisola was out after them. He wondered why things and people about him always had to seem heavy, rocking, hag-ridden.

Then sensing his nastiness he dreamt he was cursing the birdsong.

Masa was expecting bad luck: her oil-lamp had upset as the cotter-pin had come out.

She sat down on the hearth-stone, still warm though the fire was dead, wringing her hands in the petticoats sunk between her thighs, rubbing her eyelids and palping her stomach, where she felt something heavy lay.

Hearing Orsola's step she called out, for all she wanted to keep it to herself:

– Know what I've done?

– No. What have you done?

Masa moved her lips without speaking.

– Out with it. Don't keep me guessing. Why did you call me?

– I've spilt the oil.

– You're joking.

– I'm not like you! I can't joke about those sort of things!

– I can't either. You'll have to watch out.

Masa could have slapped her face. Holding her head down Orsola was trying to think what was the bad luck Masa might have.

– And I don't think I've done anything wrong.

– But you know these things happen to anyone. Remember when the fox chopped the broody hen I forgot to shut indoors? I'd spilt the oil then. And if that wasn't enough my husband was going to beat me!

Masa stroked her cheek with her palm. Orsola scratched her breasts, her bunched fist making the whole bodice move forward. She said:

– Don't worry. Come and tell me what happens. I'm dying to know too.

And she left her.

Masa went to meet Giacco and Ghisola to make sure they'd not dropped dead in the fields. She didn't tell Giacco so as not to get scolded. Ghisola reacted with superstitious terror. She wouldn't go into her room in the dark to change her pinny.

She set on her knees a nest with five baby sparrows in it, taken from a poplar she'd climbed, and began cramming the fledglings' gaping beaks with breadcrumbs. She'd been going to rear them but excited by her terror had an urge to kill them. Two or three had their eyes shut, one suddenly lifted its wings but fell over, another underneath cheeped without stop.

So she squashed their heads together in her fingers and frizzled them in the skillet. Refusing to taste them Masa tried to think of something else and appealed to the smoke-stained crucifix. She sat shaking her head and kept peeking round the door.

Spot crawled under the table and sniffed at each of the chairs in turn, brushing his tail against the linen cloth, then went out.

What could it mean, this sniffing round the room? Grandmother and granddaughter exchanged glances.

But nothing unlucky happened and after supper Orsola said to Masa:

– You're out of danger now.

She was envious and checking the oil really had been spilt thought to herself: *She has all the luck!*

Ghisola stood at the window, now and then dragging spits over something it was too dark for her to make out. For a while she looked up at the sky, where more and more stars had been appearing.

A damp strip of sepia-coloured cloud split the cobalt vault from the horizon glowing under the declining sunrays. The olive-trees' foliage looked like a single veil held in place by the splayed branches and enveloping every tree.

The cypresses beside the threshing-floor were black.

21

Midges and moths brushed the girl's forehead and an unfamiliar fragrance alternated with the warm stink from the byre underneath.

From a peach-tree in blossom, moist and gummy, a cicada shrilled once, as if it had dreamt of something.

Flour! How well Masa knew what it was and what it cost: the stuff that stuck to her fingers and was kept locked in the meal-chest with almost religious reverence.

She ate slices of bread like a boy from upcountry tasting his first lolly and afraid it will finish too soon. Not touching it with her lips she bit bits off with a meticulous movement of the whole mouth and while swallowing kept her eyes fixed on the piece held in her hand and her legs crossed.

Flour was what she and all her family were. Giacco used to say:

– Aren't we made of bread too?

When he plunged his bare arm into a sack of corn, to make sure it wasn't warming up, the grains seemed to be trying to scamper round it. Masa would ask:

– Have the weevils got in?

– You'd rather get your hide tanned, wouldn't you?

Masa flushed, but her mind was eased.

Agostino, the son of a horse-coper who had two farms adjoining Poggio a' Meli, didn't like Pietro to talk to

Ghisola too much. He had the adolescent conceit that's like sexual jealousy. And he realized Ghisola must hate Pietro's naive respect for her, despise it as a weakness.

Ghisola did in fact make the young master feel awkward but he wanted to be big and tried to persuade himself he preferred being friends with Agostino. He gave in to his wishes, doing what he told him to do and trying to guess what he was thinking but didn't say straight out. Sometimes he fetched him a pebble, demanded with a glance, to fling at a bird just spotted on a wayside bough. How Agostino's shirt swelled in the breeze when it was all undone! Why didn't he have arms like his, and eyebrows and ears like his, and a shirt like that? And why, trying to behave in the same carefree way, did he quail and pant, afraid of provoking anger that made him tremble? Why couldn't he stand up to the pained look in those lustrous unfathomable eyes, when he tried to disregard his demands or hadn't guessed right? That look scared him, like when you come unawares on a spring gushing right at your feet.

Agostino had a small boy's snub nose covered with freckles but a neck like a lady's and shapely hands. His talks with Ghisola, consisting of senseless catchphrases only the two of them understood, roused in Pietro unexpected feelings unlike any he'd have dreamt of on his own. It was such fun to listen to them! He seemed to learn something too.

Ghisola had a pleasant smile signifying things no one else could think of and Pietro longed to know what they were, as he tried to learn the songs she sang. But he couldn't even sing and this made him ashamed. Sometimes, to stop her laughing, he did something deliberately to spite her.

Under her broad-brimmed straw always flopping over one ear, with a satin remnant for hatband and two of Anna's cast-off rosettes, Ghisola's face was placid, listless, sloppy.

In her skirt patched and cobbled she looked a simpleton, almost an idiot.

There are creatures who don't ask anything of anybody, who give everything up. Not receiving the consideration others do, others think they can do what they like with them. So they shrink from anything to do with anybody else. If someone falls in love with them they won't alter, they'll only wonder what demand is being made on them. Then they'll keep out of his way.

When Masa rapped her knuckles on Ghisola's forehead and asked *What have you got in there?* she answered pettishly:

– What do you know about it? What's it got to do with you?

At times, both pleased and put out, she thought her face gave offence. She went quiet when others talked, thinking they distrusted her. She took no interest in anything. She did as she was told, by Masa and by the master and the mistress, because left to herself she wouldn't even have thought of knitting and had a grudging sense things outside herself did exist.

Other times she seemed to be talking to the doorstep, where she used to sit.

She'd never risk having an idea because she had too many that didn't suit her, just as she never asked for the dainties she saw when she went to the restaurant. They made her hot and bothered, like the heated rooms she wasn't used to.

But she had a prescient sense of a way of life that went to her head like wealth and luxury do to others.

Living so close to Ghisola it was to her Pietro owed his first stirrings of delicacy. He admired a flower he'd picked for her on impulse but not daring to give it to her threw it away, still mistrustful of himself and feeling diminished in his own eyes. How mysterious the whole of nature suddenly seemed to be, and violent with it! Hopelessly beyond him!

He'd lain flat on his face on the ground, enclosing in his arms a day-old chick, to keep it by him. He helped ants by moving out of their way a stick they had to climb over, hesitating, then desperate, staggering under the weight of a grain too big for them to carry, so that they fell down. He cradled a ladybird in the hollow of his hand and rebuked it when it flew away!

He made attempts to subdue his fits of melancholy but couldn't put them from his mind at will. Sometimes he was jolted out of them and then his mind went into a confused and turbid state that always seemed on the point of dying away. He had the illusion it was assuming enormous proportions, so that his thoughts went astray in it and produced unexpected echoes, as in a large hall. How often he'd given himself up for lost while external images continued to stream into his brain! One minute he seemed to possess himself completely, the next less, and these shifts unsettled him, giving him dizzy spells.

Sometimes he thought he was at school when all at once in rolled a bass drum. He had such an urge to laugh he took fright, stifling the nightmare scream. Anna thought he was ill and laid a hand on his forehead:

– Feverish?

Then he did scream:

– No! No! Leave me alone!

It was a year since the night of the nightingales, another year just the same: the restaurant and the customers,

Poggio a' Meli and the farm-labourers.

At the approach of spring Domenico began making preparations for the heavier yields he expected. He visited the farm more often, a sort of reward to himself for his hard work at the restaurant. And the weather keeping fine he took Pietro with him. It did the boy good, it might set him up!

He wanted him to go afield, attend to the pruning of the vines and all the other jobs, like he did. But Pietro didn't seem to see or hear anything. So Domenico had him taken back to the threshing-floor by one of the women returning from the fields with an armful of fresh grass or the quitch cleared from a plot being dug.

One time Pietro sat down to wait for his father on Giacco's doorstep where Ghisola used to sit, unconsciously he copied her. Masa was sweeping up, using a broom-head stuck on an old brolly-handle and raising a dust so thick he could taste it. She asked him politely:

– Would you mind standing up?

He didn't budge. She stopped.

Among the motley rags, crumpled packets and coils of human hair was a doll made out of a piece of white stuff wound round a wooden spoon. Pietro had an impulse to salvage it and jumped to his feet. Masa took the chance to sweep the rubbish out through the doorway. Finishing face up the doll seemed to Pietro like a living thing. He didn't touch it. Just then Ghisola came up from the fields and seeing the doll among the sweepings kept quiet: for some time her granny had been telling her to throw it away, but pulled a weepy face. Masa shouted at her:

– Still bothered about things like that?

To tease her Pietro dug the doll into the mud with his heel, then went at it furiously, his heart palpitating, his face ashen with fear when he saw it re-emerge.

Watching him from the door Ghisola muttered:

– Fool!

Pietro felt remorse and did all he could to make it up

26

to her but she turned her back on him, munching a piece of bread she'd found in the meal-chest. Then he opened a penknife he had in his pocket and stabbed her in the thigh. She went pale but made an effort to control herself. Stung by what he took to be a deliberate slight and thinking he hadn't hurt her Pietro made another lunge with the knife but she kicked at him and ran to her room, dropping the bread. At the noise of chairs being bumped granny left off sweeping and went back indoors to see what she was up to. Ghisola could be heard whining the long whine all on one note that breaks off abruptly.

Alone in the kitchen and tittering with fright Pietro was creeping up to have a look when Masa came out and yelled:

– What did you want to make her bleed for, you wicked boy? I'm not having it. I'll tell the master.

– I couldn't help it.

Masa was beside herself and nearly clouted him over the head with something.

Convinced what he'd said was true Pietro even swore to it, using oaths he'd gone to a lot of trouble to learn and was glad of the opportunity to rehearse.

But Domenico and Anna smacked his hands in front of Masa and Ghisola and made him apologize. Though the punishment gave him something like pleasure he felt abashed a long while after, as though his pranks terrified him. He became so superstitious about it he gave up pretend-games, thinking something dreadful bound to occur sooner or later. He'd had a foretaste of it a couple of years before when, throwing a stone, he'd hurt a boy he didn't know was behind a hedge. So his talks with Ghisola assumed a sombre tone, as though there was a new meaning to them they had to hide.

A few months later, happening to see her alone in the fields he first went the other way but then turned back and made bold to ask:

– Did I hurt you at all?

His feet sinking in the turned earth gave him a sense of

discouragement. But she smiled:

– When?

– When I stuck my penknife in your leg but didn't mean to.

Already the smile had put him out, made him lose the thread.

– Still bothered about that?

He was surprised to find her attitude quite different from the one he'd supposed she'd have. He asked:

– Perhaps you'd forgot all about it?

– I forgot straightaway.

She seemed to mean: *It was one of those nasty things you don't think about.*

– But it must have really hurt. If you'd like to do the same to me . . .

– Me do it to you?

– Yes. I swear. When I swear something you know it's true. I did hurt you, didn't I?

He explained she had to stab him with the penknife, in the same place. To make out she took him seriously she answered:

– Whenever you like.

But her consent weakened his purpose.

– Nobody'd have to know about it.

– I'll say I did it myself.

He took her by the wrist to place the knife in her hand but she suddenly wriggled free, scowling with mistrust.

– Have I ever told you a lie? I'm not Agostino!

She seemed so displeased with his insistence he went away, patting the panicles of full-grown oats. He was confused but determined to stay out of her sight. He found her presence repulsive. Perhaps, he thought, it was because of her granny and aunt she wouldn't do it.

But Ghisola was sure he hadn't meant what he'd said. She had an aversion to the master's son, the instinctive spiteful aversion of those obliged to obey.

28

In any case she was inclined to think him insincere as this gave her another reason for disliking him. Whenever she saw him from a distance and he was too shy even to look in her direction she burst out singing.

At school Pietro chaffed the boys next him, pestering them with his nervous gaiety, demanding their attention, calling them funny names, provoking them if they ignored him. Even when they were all quiet he just didn't hear the teacher, though any answer from a classmate reached his ears, sounding curiously melancholy.

The biggest in the school and the bottom of his class, he was due to take the leaving exam. The seminarists taunted him.

Sometimes after making an effort to understand he forced himself to attend to the rest of the lesson and took a kind of pleasure in increasing everyone's disrespect for him, though he complained of it. Concentration left him with his brain strained, a weight between his temples, incapable of settling down to his homework, worn out with nothing done. He put one book aside and took up another, put that aside too and stopped reading, not even noticing he still had the books there.

At those times the bustle and babble of the restaurant distracted him.

On top of it all he was supposed to prepare his lessons and do his writing in front of the less well-to-do customers who had their meals at a long table where each spread a small place-cloth. Pietro took pinches of the bread-crumbs that lodged along their folds.

These customers had become friendly with his parents and they teased him with little jokes:

– What are you trying your eyes for? Run away and play.

But Anna would rise from her easy-chair, positioned in the darkest corner behind a wooden divider with a round peep-hole, from where she could keep an eye on the waiters and the girl serving wine:

– Let him alone!

Then she'd laugh too.

In summer, whenever there was a breath of air, you could see all the smoke from the pipes and cigars waft out of the open window. Then the customers took off their jackets, whereas in winter they passed round an earthenware pipkin containing hot embers to warm their hands.

They played tricks on one another, snitching bread and fruit. When one of them swore too hard Anna turned pale and stared him in the face. He bit back what he'd been going to say and the others hushed, then the subject was changed.

– Swearing's not decent. You can do that outside. In the street.

The man went red:

– It wasn't me you told off yesterday, was it ma'am?

There was a spontaneous burst of laughter and Anna immediately thought of something else.

Then one of them would make a suggestion:

– Let's have a drink. But not that watery stuff. Don't take it out on us!

Those who had heeltaps drained their glasses and placed them with the others in the centre of the table. Anna ordered up a flask and asked each one in turn:

– How much do you want?

– One soldo.

– I want two.

Adamo held his glass to the daylight:

– The cellar ceiling's been leaking again!

When a customer walked by from one of the other rooms they went as quiet as they could and watched him pass:

– It's so-and-so.

Sometimes they sang. But Domenico would come out of the kitchen carrying a ladle of hot stock and they'd all throw up their hands:

– Steady! Steady! We're just going.

Quarrels were few and when they occurred rifts were shortlived. Ordinarily they didn't bandy insults direct. One at a time each would address the others, setting out the matter like a story, first quietly, then vehemently and in strong language, brandishing his fists and rising in his seat.

The disputants would be nearly at blows when someone would say:

– Disgraceful! People can hear us!

That was enough for Anna and the stream of oaths would be brought to an end with a big gulp.

When Adamo, simpering like a spoilt girl, asked Domenico to see he was well looked after, it was like begging a favour. He'd look into his face then turn aside and wait, always with a fear they'd be calling him names in the kitchen. Taking two or three tastes, if the dish was to his liking he breathed deep, hawked and fell to. His cheerfulness restored, he was the first to wake Giacomino by putting apple-peel inside his collar. Elderly short and stout, for ever gnawing his moustache, his moods were as changeable as a child's. He'd apologize for an impoliteness of the moment before, drumming on his place-cloth and holding his head forward and down. He'd stroke his cheeks with the back of his hands, in silence, chewing his cigar and rolling it between his lips. He could settle himself to listen to a long discussion in the next room, giving his opinion in a single remark or a sigh. If he received an answer he'd sink back in thought, taking longer pulls at his cigar.

Even while eating Giacomino rested his head on his hands, tugging at the hairs near the nape of his neck.

Bibe would prop his chin on his fist at the table's edge

31

and sit in that position with his eyes down, amusing himself by listening without looking at anyone. Then he'd quietly lift his toes, one foot after the other, beating time with them till someone seized him by his curly hair and twisted his neck round.

– God! That hurt! What do you think you're playing at?
– Sleepy, you pig?
– Rather.

And he told them why he'd not had his sleep out, grinning drowsily.

They always wanted the same seats: Adamo in a corner because there he could spit as much as he liked, Giacomino under the window and Bibe, the youngest, on the settle, because he could lean back on it, as his habit was, even go to sleep there when left undisturbed.

They rebuttoned their trousers, rebuckled their belts, spat, jostled, cuffed one another about the head, tugged their moustaches and paid their bills, one at a time going up to Anna's cubby-hole.

And Pino? Pino, the old tranter of Poggibonso, the poorest of them all. He'd call out, joking:

– Any room for me?

They all made room for him, not out of politeness but because they thought he was crummy. He noticed but didn't dare say anything, muttering a little to himself. Being treated like that wherever he went he didn't take offence.

– Half a seat's enough for me. I'm no gentleman. Oh my bones do ache!

One of his eyes wouldn't stay open but blinked its lids together like owls do theirs. He swept the other all round the room, slowly and always starting again from the same point. He examined his hands to show he'd not forgotten to wash them: actually he'd swilled them in the horse-pail. The horse was half done for, so were the shafts of the cart, strengthened with several turns of string or wire. What a time those repairs took, renewed every day!

He rubbed his eyes with one finger, smiling vacantly, the smile making his mouth look twice as wide.

– You're laughing, you old rascal! What have you nicked today? You take the stuff they give you to deliver and then say it got lost on the road.

– Would I do that? Poor fellow! I used to once but I don't now.

He drawled, with intonations that sounded sincere yet sly.

– I've got two girls at home to marry off. Really lovely girls they are, between you and me. But my wife's just a bundle of greasy rags you wouldn't soil your hands with. I've got those two girls, poor kids! What am I to do for them?

His whole face took on a look of humble but stubborn goodness. Curious, in between the hairs of his thin beard the skin of his cheeks was as delicate as a woman's.

He didn't place an order but Domenico picked out scraps from the day before and made him up a single dish. Then he'd pull his hat-brim down till it almost covered his nose:

– Smell what I've brought you?

– I do. It's stale but it doesn't smell bad.

Adamo and Giacomino flipped over slices of bread or sleepy fruit. Without looking them in the face he gathered it in with both hands as if he meant to put it right under his plate.

– Oh I feel better today!

Anna he greeted with great respect, waiting for her to answer: he'd never think of sitting down first. So that when she forgot she had to say:

– Do sit down!

– So I can sit down? I was afraid I was being a nuisance today. I'm so tired!

He waited, holding his hands together.

About once a month he got Pietro to explain what the two oleographs hanging on the wall were. Pietro stood on the bench to save taking them down. But Pino said:

– Bring them nearer! If you only knew, Pietrino, my eyes smart so. Sometimes I'm afraid I'll go blind.

One was *The battle of Adowa* and the other *The makers of Italian unity*. Afterwards, holding him by his sleeve:

– Never mind what your pa says. Work at your books. I know what I'm talking about!

Pietro stroked his hand, not knowing why.

In winter, seeing him starved with cold and wet through, his coat-collar turned up to the tips of his ears and his hat pulled down over his eyes, Pietro suddenly went up to him and without saying anything put his face so close to Pino's, Domenico yanked him back by the neck.

He died soon after. Nobody took any notice.

A year later: it was late March, St Joseph's day.

From Poggio a' Meli you could hear the bells, remixing in the sky and pealing pellmell, the sound getting louder and louder but hardly moving, with a deep boom. An uncharacteristic gaiety had come over Pietro, a gaiety like an excess of well-being that tensed his nerves.

Let me talk about these March turbulences, impossible to describe exactly and nearly always associated with a subtle sensual pleasure, a thirst for beauty.

Those self-doubting gleams of sunshine, those twitterings as yet out of sight and soon out of mind, those fleecy clouds that seem to have come ahead of their time! Dead leaves still lying on germinating seed, mixing pallor of death with paleness of life! Leaves of all species still lying on sprouting grass, lopped trees, their brash scattered over the ground, to be taken away, for ever! Dead wood cut from fruit-trees still reluctant to blossom on the new growth! The soil tacky, sticking to the blades of spades so that men have to clean it off with the ball of the thumb, and the clods on their wooden clogs! And the almost matrimonial and to us unknowable love the creatures have that do things for each other, and their hates too! Mistletoe springing from espalier boughs, slashed off with a bill-hook! It will regrow at once. Chestnut buds!

Domenico went afield followed by his labourers to arrange the next day's jobs.

Pietro had filled out but was pale with a sickly look. He was just fourteen. He thought his jacket with the sailor collar, cut for economy out of an old dress, silly and wrong for his age.

He slipped inside Giacco's. Giacco as usual clapped a hand on his shoulder.

– How you've shot up! Bet you've brought me some baccy.

Pietro seized the points of his moustache and pulled them first one way, then the other, Giacco swivelling his neck sharp so as not to get hurt.

The boy laughed, looking at Masa. She said:

– Harder.

– No no. That's enough.

Giacco eased him off firmly. Then he asked:

– Not one butt then?

Rebecca saved the cigar-stumps she found sweeping the restaurant and gave them to Pietro to take to him.

Masa spoke up again.

– Master Pietro doesn't smoke.

She laughed with him as if it was a joke. After laughing she twisted her lips and bit them. The old man took from his weskit pocket a chipped cutty-pipe with a stem that fitted into his palm.

– Thank goodness I've still got some his mother gave me last week. See if I haven't!

He tapped the pipe on the table-edge and an ashy powder dropped out. He gathered it together, stirred it and put it back in the bowl. Then from the fire he took a burning stick. There stole out of his mouth a wisp of smoke, pale blue. He watched it go and said:

– Ah, not much fine cut these days!

With a stubbed thumbnail chopped in an accident when he was young he tamped the smoulder into the bowl.

Again Pietro saw the wisp of smoke and in his mind's eye, as if it was real and made him feel sick, his mother going to a drawer in the house to get something out. Everyone had gone away! But as she kept trying to pull it out the drawer vanished into the wall. Then he seemed to feel her hands on his face giving him a big kiss, her hands kissing him.

Masa was astonished at the look of fright on his face and asked:

– What are you thinking about?

Giacco went to the door and said:

– I've got to see to the cows. Let me have the rope.

But worried by the young master's look Masa answered grumpily:

– Where did you put it?

And Giacco:

– Find it for me.

– You never know what you do with anything. Then you need your wife to get it for you.

– Stop nagging. You'd do better to find me the rope instead of answering me back.

– I'll nag as much as I like. As much as you do.

Then she asked Pietro, to take his mind off some reproof she thought might be troubling him:

– Have you seen Ghisola today?

Heedlessly he answered:

– Isn't she here?

– She was going to mass in Siena.

Said Giacco, in the tone of one renewing an argument. But Masa stood up for her:

– It was a good idea. Here at Poggio a' Meli you never see anybody.

And to Pietro she went on:

– I thought you might have met her.

The old couple became thoughtful, casting each other glances Pietro didn't understand. With a sigh Masa exclaimed:

– It will be as God wills.

– What will? asked Pietro. Tell me.

He was filled with a keen curiosity.

– Where is she? Is she coming back soon?

He was alarmed. It showed in his blue eyes, so candid everyone could always tell. The eyelids felt like warm water.

The horse, harnessed to the gig tied to an iron ring in the yard, had turned to one side to rest. Spot was finishing off a muddy crust, holding it still with his paws the better to gnaw it.

Pietro hadn't yet calmed down when he caught sight of Ghisola.

She had grown into a young woman. Her black eyes were like two olives, the two on the twig you see first because they're the best. She was slender and had thin lips.

He was carried away. She walked at a leisurely pace with slight movements of the head and her jet-black oil-sleeked hair was done a different way, unlike any before.

She tried to stop smiling, lowering her head, but slowed down as if undecided whether or not to keep a secret. He felt a sharp resentment and took a step towards her as he used to when they were smaller, to tease her or tell her something, meaning to take her down a peg.

How much prettier she was since he'd seen her last!

Jealously he noted a red hair-ribbon, boots shining with cart-grease and a beige dress nearly new. He heaved a sigh.

But angrier than he'd ever thought she could possibly be she cried out:

– Go away. There's your father. Don't come near me.

Still he came on. She slewed round, brushing against him but not getting touched. Pietro didn't say anything, didn't even look at her. He was hurt, humiliated. Why was she carrying on like that? He'd go and see her indoors: she'd gone in, first pausing with one foot on the doorstep. His inside melted and he felt stirred by something he didn't understand, he had a desire to impose himself on her.

By degrees he calmed down and recovered his spirits, while a delicious sensation made itself felt more and more.

Ghisola soon came out again. She'd taken off the ribbon, changed her boots and put on a faded red apron. Lifting her eyes at Pietro she gravely and silently shimmied into the barn. Into a basket she put some hay her grandfather had cut, then stopped to extract a splinter from her finger. He felt just like that hand. Her silence baffled and embarrassed him, nothing would have enabled him to speak first. So he gave her a slight push and she frowned, pretending to nearly fall over.

He said:

– Next time I'll knock you down good and proper!

– Just you try!

When she wanted it to her voice became hard and harsh, squawking like a hen. He looked at her with annoyance, feeling she was supposed to defer to him.

Lovers don't usually hear the sound of the other's voice while talking. At least they couldn't describe it.

She added:

– Go away.

The effect on him was like when we hold our heads under water and can't keep our eyes open but he answered:

– Ghisola, a month ago you told me you loved me. Don't you remember? I remember and I love you too.

And he laughed, ending in an articulate babble. Ghisola looked at him as if he amused her. Indeed she liked his dodge, making something up to say something that was true.

She answered:

– I know, I know.

38

But he couldn't continue. Instead he noticed how dainty the pocket of her apron was. From it he suddenly snatched a small hanky roughly hemmed with pale blue wool.

– Give it back.

Afraid he'd blundered he gave it back to her.

– Did you prick your finger?

He thought it quite an achievement, managing to say something.

– What do you care? You don't do any work. You never do anything.

She had answered with an arrogant jeer but he took her seriously.

– I'll help you if you like, Ghisola.

She pretended to tease him, making out he wasn't able to, and held him off, saying he wanted to touch her, not help her.

Domenico came up from the fields.

Pietro hurriedly picked up an olive-twig and began sweeping the barn doorway as though to kill the ants crossing it in single file.

Ghisola bent down to grab handfuls of the hay, turning aside from the heap with quick jerks till the basket was filled. Then she lifted it to hitch it onto her shoulder but couldn't do it by herself. The bones of her forearms looked like putting her elbows out.

Pietro helped her before his father could see. While lending support to his actions Ghisola kept Domenico under watch with her sharp black eyes, the eyelids with an edge on them like the midribs some grassblades have. But Pietro blushed and trembled because before moving away she took him by the hand. He was amazed, feeling such a sweetness go through him he nearly fainted. He thought: *That's what it must be like.*

Checking by feel the buckles of the horse's harness Domenico called out to him:

– You there unharness him and turn him round. Fold up the blanket and put it on the seat.

The horse wouldn't turn round and the transom jammed. The look in Spot's eyes, always angry, also confused Pietro.

– Pull him towards you!

He had no strength left. He couldn't get a grip on the bridle and his fingers slid into the bit, slobbery with nasty green saliva. All the same he did his best, knowing Ghisola must be there, back from the byre. His trembling got worse. The horse's hoofs touched him, trod on him.

Domenico seized the whip and advancing on Pietro raised it to his nose.

– I know what's the matter with you. But I'll make something of you yet.

Ghisola came to the gig and helped him, after stopping at the corner of the well to scrape a clog clean of dung from the byre.

Still holding the whip Domenico went to have a word with Giacco, who listened with his arms dangling and his thumbs stuck in his fists, the veins ridging the skin like earthworms lying in mud.

Pietro hadn't the courage to look Ghisola in the face. Her eyes now followed him everywhere. He sagged at the knees with a new weakness that increased his confusion like a disease. Ghisola helped him again. Taking hold of the red blanket that had been spread over the horse's back her fingers touched his and laying it on the seat their knuckles knocked together. Both turned faint but felt like laughing.

Domenico clambered onto the gig, darted a look at Pietro and shouted again:

– Get a move on! What's that you've got on your underlip? Wipe it off.

Scared, Pietro answered:

– Nothing.

Then he thought there might be a mark left by what he'd said to Ghisola. Immediately after he was sorry he'd been so foolish, while his heart jumped like it was trying to get out.

Giacco and the farm-labourers doffed their hats. Pietro just had time to make a little signal to Ghisola with the corner of his mouth but her mind was on the master and she frowned quickly. Then Pietro fixed his gaze on the horse's head. It was already pulling out of the yard, breaking into a trot as soon as it got on the road.

From the sun setting behind the Montagnola light more red than pink spread over Siena. But it was the cypresses dotted about, in lines or rings on the hilltops, that filled him with regret for being removed from something immense.

Domenico never spoke while driving, acknowledging greetings with a nod. But he grinned at an occasional girl he knew: slackening the horse's pace he'd touch her in the middle of her apron with the tip of his whip. Pietro, his eyes half-closed, turned the other way, blushing. He then amused himself by watching the movement of the horse's hoofs. The metre of their clopping seemed to vary with the tunes going on in his head. Or he tried not to smell that smell his father's clothes had.

Pietro had grown so idle at school, by May the rector wouldn't keep him on.

Domenico strapped him with his trouser-belt till he made Anna cry too. But next day nobody said any more about it.

Anna explained to Rebecca:

– It's our enemies putting curses on us.

Every day she said some prayers to a saint but never found it possible to have a serious talk about Pietro with her husband. He always answered:

– Not today. I'm busy.

If she tried to hold him back by his coat he'd go off

41

saying:

– See about him yourself. You too now . . .

More she didn't dare do, afraid he'd start on Pietro again, pummel him silly, making out he'd lost control.

Nor was it possible at night. As soon as she started talking about him he'd clench his fists and cry out:

– Let me sleep. I'm tired. I've been working since morning. You must rest too . . .

Or he answered:

– Have you cashed up today? You must check the till before you come to bed. It's necessary.

If she retorted with silence he'd lift her head from the pillow:

– Answer me!

He'd wait awhile, trying to argue, but then fall asleep.

During one of their disputes in the restaurant Pietro cut in:

– I'm going to learn drawing.

A lawyer's clerk who'd just finished his lunch guffawed.

Pietro gave him a long stare, dumbfounded to see the mild contented eyes looking down on him.

He was a fat man with a shiny crimson face studded with warts. He wore a light-coloured suit with a gold watch-chain: fair hair, low forehead. With calm self-assurance he said to Domenico:

– Take no notice of him. Teach him your trade. Restaurants just rake it in.

Everybody laughed. He meant the bill he had to pay.

His face tingling from chin to scalp Pietro burst out:

– What's it got to do with you?

The clerk drew from a leather case an amber gold-ringed holder and into it fitted a half-smoked cigar. Then he said:

– Go and buy me a box of matches.

And he threw a copper on the table.

Pietro looked at his father. All eyes were turned on him, their eyes and faces seared his soul. His heart pounded. Domenico said:

– Go along then!

He snatched up the money and ran to the tobacconist's.

The clerk laughed so hard his face turned puce. In between spasms of coughing he added:

– Make him do what he's told as much as you can.

Anna resented these familiarities but didn't retaliate in case it should lose custom. But they excited Domenico and made him more opinionated than ever. To Pietro he'd say:

– Mark my words. There's no need for you to do any more school-work. All you need to know is your tables. Schools ought to be done away with and the teachers sent out to dig. That's the best thing God has given us: land.

Displeased, Anna would answer:

– Those are your ideas.

And Domenico would ask with scorn:

– And how long were you at school?

That was all he needed, for his wife to turn against him! She shook her head.

– We can't even write our names but we've got on.

The customers would sit thoughtful and then exclaim, to spare Anna's feelings:

– He's young yet. There's no knowing what you might make of him.

– But when I'm sixty and he's over twenty I'll still be able to give him a thrashing.

– Oh he won't grow up as big and strong as you are, that's for sure!

Lunch each had whenever he could find time after his chores were done but in the evening they all ate together. Domenico at the head of the table, Pietro between him and Rebecca. Facing the boss sat the cook and on the remaining side of the table the two waiters. The kitchen-help sat by himself at a fly-table also used to put plates and cutlery on but at an angle, so that he didn't turn his back on the others. Anna stayed in her easy-chair as there she could see if a customer came in.

The cook had gone to the kitchen-doorway to smoke a cigar-butt, leaning his head and shoulders against the wall, the cellar-girl was carrying plates and the kitchen-help, skipping like a boy, ran to tell the stableman to put the horse to.

Domenico downed another glass of wine and then took out his false teeth to wipe them in his napkin, furtively, keeping his hands under the table.

Anna took up a shirt to do some mending.

Finally, with a flick of his place-cloth, Domenico swept the crumbs off his trousers and got Rebecca to brush him down and Tiburzi to buff his boots, giving a few orders while they were at it. He tittuped behind his son, who was drumming on a windowpane to accompany the humming he was making with his lips, slapped him round the neck and said:

– Come to the farm with me.

Without answering Pietro jumped into the gig, already hitched up, and they were at Poggio a' Meli just before sunset.

Turning a corner of the barn Ghisola saw him standing on the threshing-floor, alone and stock-still, his hands in his pockets. She ticked him off in earnest:

– What are you doing here? Why haven't you been before? For you it used to be wonderful. But I don't care.

She added:

44

– I know what you want to tell me.

He thought: *Yes, she knows. The others know all about me. I'm the one who doesn't.*

That inner life of his that always got on top! How it drove him to despair, not being able to savour till afterwards, in his own private silence, all he'd experienced but hadn't said! It was why he considered himself inferior to the others. He only talked well to Ghisola in his imagination, chiefly when he'd just woken up.

His self-consciousness increased. His collar was making his chin itch.

Ghisola looked at him as if he tickled her too. He began kicking at an olive-tree to make her stop. But when he raised his eyes again she was looking at him harder than ever, mouth open in mockery. No doubt now!

The sun went down and a shiver ran over him. He couldn't stand that grin any more, he wanted to forget he'd ever seen it. He dropped his head again, thinking he ought to understand why he disliked it.

Ghisola titivated her hair, holding the hairpins in her open hand to let him see they were new. Before resetting each one she pricked his hand with it but he didn't move.

Tufts of grass bent over as insects hopped onto the tips of the blades.

When Ghisola pricked him Pietro thought; *She knows what I want all right. But I'd have to tell her. It's necessary.*

Her scarlet stockings emboldened him but unable to utter a word he approached her almost trembling.

In between the olive-trees they could only just see each other and the ground was already umber.

– What do you want? Tell me from where you are. Don't come too near.

Ghisola noticed he didn't take his eyes off her stockings but her skirt being short she couldn't hide them.

– You know.

Her face became soft and bashful.

– You know? Tell me then.

45

A blush suffused her face, altering its expression.

– I know.

And as he was getting nearer she fended him off with her thin hard hands.

Pietro was so frantic he nearly tottered. Ghisola's eyes were still fixed on him. He saw nothing but those eyes and all the shadow behind her together with the olive-grove seemed to be moving in time with his movements.

– Let me go now. We'll talk about it another time . . . Another time I said!

The dusk seemed to disembody him, swallow him up.

Ghisola whispered:

– I love you.

And off she ran, round the other side of the barn: the master was making his way towards the threshing-floor in his huge boots, breathing heavily and bobbing his head up and down. Pietro stayed where he was, chipping the corner of the barn with a stone he'd come upon in his pocket. He was getting his knuckles grazed but didn't feel it.

Domenico looked on and had a laugh with Enrico, the labourer following him.

– Are you crazy? What do you think you're doing there, messing the wall up?

Then to the labourer:

– That slut got away sharp enough anyhow!

– They're both still kids. I think they just play.

He spoke up for them, supposing the master favoured Giacco and Masa. But glad of the chance to snub him Domenico answered:

– I know better. Shut up.

Then Enrico agreed:

– They'd soon be at it!

And gulped, as he always did after saying anything.

His father's rebuke had intimidated Pietro. He'd already put Ghisola out of his mind, though there remained a fascination he couldn't resist. He started walking towards

Domenico, who'd taken the horse by the bridle and was turning it towards the road.

– Get in.

He obeyed, trying to clean his grubby hands and not looking anyone in the face.

The horse wouldn't stand still in front of the open gate and Domenico began whipping it above the knees. The horse backed, rearing its forelegs, and the gig bumped into the wall.

– Whoa. You've got to learn. Or else . . .

He gave it a cut of the whip.

– If you won't do as you're told either . . .

And he gave it another cut of the whip.

– I'll teach you a lesson. Stand still.

He reversed the whip and struck the horse across its nostrils with the stock. The horse tossed its head and Pietro made to get down.

– Stay where you are. If you get down I'll whip you too.

The labourers looked on uneasily. They were impatient for the master to go, afraid he'd turn on them, abuse them, perhaps even take it into his head he could whip them as well.

The horse stood still.

Domenico gave Pietro the whip to hold and facing the horse buttoned his coat up.

– I mean to be obeyed, mind. You're standing still now, see? I'll take my time, then I'll get in.

To test it he undid his coat-buttons and did them up again, pausing whenever the horse moved its head.

He readjusted one of the reins and made to get in, stopping with one foot on the footboard. Then, holding onto the gig by his hands, he swung himself up and dropped beside Pietro, shouting:

– Move over.

Pietro was mentally blocked and didn't stir.

– Move across, you fool!

And suddenly to the labourers:

47

– Do the jobs I've given you or I'll sack the lot of you. Those strips have got to be dug by tomorrow.

– Yes sir.

– You can depend on us.

– As if we couldn't, with all of us to dig and all day to do it in!

– So long as it doesn't rain!

Domenico looked at the one who'd said that as if he was going to hurl himself on top of him. In a voice like chisel striking stone he said:

– If it rains you'll bottle the wine. Giacco, you'll hand out the vat-house keys. That's what you've got them for.

– Yes sir. Right sir.

Finally he remembered the restaurant, looked at his watch, saw he couldn't delay any longer and left.

The sunset had been brief and overcast, with the clouds that bring rain. Pietro kept his hands in his pockets, thinking he'd be whistling if he'd been by himself. In the dark all the horse's hoofs seemed to be clopping in unison. Domenico drove, vexed he hadn't told the labourers to make the holes for the olive-trees. Afraid his orders wouldn't be carried out with anxious attention to detail he seemed to follow in his mind everything they did. It maddened him he couldn't be beside them all the time. In his eagerness to catch them out he sometimes lost his temper and became more violent still.

He thought of turning back to make sure none of them was dawdling in the yard, perhaps even talking about him. He glanced up at the clouds and felt he'd like to flog them, send them packing.

Meanwhile a morbid notion had come into Pietro's mind that horse and gig were being dragged backwards into an ever-widening cavern of his soul.

All at once, in a sudden involuntary movement where he smelt the taste in his mouth, he moaned and stretched his head forward as if about to fall off.

Domenico shouted at him:

48

– What's the matter?

He thought Pietro was falling asleep and was going to give him a punch.

The Vico Alto cypresses snagged the sky. The Porta Camollia was ruddy and deep inside the city the first street-lamp was switched on.

The trees along the avenue and on the top of the railway embankment moved by in silence, their foliage set off against mountains of the purest purple. The Osservanza looked benign.

Beyond the roofs of the Via Camollia the top of the Mangia Tower rose in the sky, white, almost radiant, but the bell with its iron frame blacker.

When Anna'd had her convulsions she'd lie back in her easy-chair, in the restaurant, all day long. Her face went white and Rebecca, who looked after her when she was ill, unlaced her stays. But there was always something the staff had to ask and then she'd open her eyes, stare into space and, shivering from head to foot, give the answer. To save her husband worry she wouldn't go to bed. But what distressed her at those times was not being able to look after Pietro.

She seemed to herself not to belong to life any more, never to have done anything for him. And then the kind of calm material comfort brings was spoilt for her by memories of her poverty. She used to say:

– It's not possible to be as happy as we'd like to be.

Her weariness of life so embittered her, she was afraid she'd not feel good ever again. The sense of death was always present and it wasn't enough for her to believe in God.

49

She took to looking at Pietro with this in mind and felt a disquiet amounting to alarm.

After being jarred by the convulsion her nerves still had a sort of sensation of pain not relieved, as she was used to having to get better unaided, never believing others could do anything for her.

Still, she hoped to recover, not that she trusted the doctor but because she'd got Pietro.

She didn't know how to talk to him. She realized he was growing away from her and without her being able to tell him any of the things it would have cheered her to say. Even when she had him near her they remained twain, mutually incomprehensible.

Pietro always avoided showing her he loved her in case he became too submissive, while she despaired beyond reason of any prank he got up to. So he was afraid when she fussed and she, prevented from giving effect to her concern, next time tried to impose it on him:

– You've got no respect for your mother!

That exasperated him and he made off, not listening even.

Anna wept when she told Rebecca, who asked with a faint smile:

– Why take on so?

As she'd nursed him and wanted him to feel affection for her too, it rather pleased her. Never noticing this Anna would answer:

– It's not for you to make excuses for him.

– Isn't it?

Rebecca bridled.

When he saw his mother crying Pietro thought she was doing it to spite him and felt like doing something worse.

Anna used to advise Rebecca and Masa how to bring Ghisola up but it was the benevolence of a mistress: that way Ghisola too came to depend on her goodwill. Yet she did have some consideration for her, like telling Masa not to work her too hard or every year giving her for handsel a new frock, bought off one of the stalls stationed at the restaurant door.

Then Ghisola would fetch her a bunch of flowers, going so far as to steal them, and wish her a happy New Year.

When villagers from Domenico's old home visited Siena they always ate at his restaurant, bringing greetings and family news, perhaps fruit done up in a bundle.

One of them, wanting his son Antonio to learn brick-laying, a trade not followed at Civitella, asked Domenico to take him under his wing and get him placed with a good builder. Sundays and holidays Domenico invited Antonio to keep Pietro company. So the two boys, who were about the same age, had to be friends though they didn't hit it off and Agostino, who couldn't stand Antonio, was ousted.

The walks they took nearly always brought them to Poggio a' Meli, as Domenico meant them to, and after a couple of months Antonio boasted he'd had a talk with Ghisola in private. It was true but at first Pietro supposed he was lying and he was staggered, the disillusion shattered his self-esteem. A friend ought not to lie. What had he said to Ghisola? And why had he talked to her without telling him first?

How humiliating it was when others trampled on his feelings, dissolved his very soul!

The others did just as they pleased with him. His throat constricted with emotion. He blushed, got flustered, felt lost. Nothing was right for him: the roads tiring, the sun hot, his clothes ill-cut, his hands too big. He strove not to think about it, to convince himself of the contrary. He was stunned, his ears buzzed and any moment he thought he'd fall down.

51

His face seemed unable to hide his frank and dogged honesty and the outrage this did to his feelings made him sick. He felt weakened by the mental anxiety he was trying to alter.

On one of those Sunday walks he again went to Poggio a' Meli with Antonio: he'd declared he'd show him up for a liar in front of Ghisola herself. But he was ashamed to tell Antonio what he suffered inwardly and felt so diminished beside him his friend did actually look taller than usual.

Even on the way they'd quarrelled, thumping each other on the back, though he'd sooner have stopped and sobbed, dismayed to see the other was amused.

Easily noticing Pietro's disquiet Antonio cried out:

– You'll see if it's not true!

Pietro didn't answer and his friend added:

– I talked to her again the other day. She promised she'd love me and not you.

To cut argument short he threw him a punch but Pietro parried it.

Increasingly sure of himself Antonio went on repeating:

– You won't get anywhere near her.

– You won't either.

– I'll do what I like.

Shamming anger he stepped up to him again with white spit coming out of his mouth. Even when he wasn't talking you could see all his upper teeth, sound but set awry. It looked like he'd planted them in his lip. And his nose was crooked.

In an attempt to win him over with kindness Pietro said:

– Then I'll be cross with you.

– As if I cared! Do what you like. Your father's friends with me and I'll come whenever I want to. He likes bringing me to the farm better than you.

Pietro felt disarmed, defenceless: it was quite true what he'd said!

They walked on side by side. After a little Antonio

stopped him, holding him back by the arm to look him in the face. He broke into a horse-laugh:

– Got nothing to say for yourself?

He spat on the grass, wiping his mouth with the back of his hand.

Pietro said:

– I'm going back.

– I'm not. I want to have that talk. You go.

– You come back too.

He wanted to prevent him from seeing her. But Antonio was going on, so Pietro had to too.

When they reached the threshing-floor Ghisola was just coming out, going afield to call her grandfather in, passing beside the big cherry-tree at the end of a vine-row.

Antonio hurried towards her to show off. But Ghisola smiled more at Pietro and indicated it was him she was stopping for.

Then Antonio went off to pick cherries, leaving them together, and Pietro asked her:

– Is it true you don't love anybody else? Tell me. If it isn't . . .

She answered gently:

– Only you. But Antonio wouldn't like . . .

That made him feel unsure and he glanced at his friend's back.

Ghisola noticed and added:

– Don't you believe me?

She shook her head. This time she spoke with so deep a calm he was reassured at once.

– But don't let him see. Why do you bring him?

She seemed to be reproaching him for not being alone with her. He thought she found this hurtful.

But her beauty dazed him and made him forget what Antonio had said.

Meanwhile Antonio had rejoined them, obviously having thought up some plan, spitting way out the stones of the cherries he'd eaten all at one go, a finger poked into his mouth. Shuddering Pietro snatched a cherry-bob hanging from Antonio's fingers. Antonio exclaimed:

– Why take them from me? Give them to Ghisola.

Pietro didn't know what to answer. He would rather not have been told what to do and stood there holding the cherries. Ghisola rescued him:

– I'll pick some for myself.

How kind and clever he thought she was!

But Antonio wasn't discouraged:

– If you can't reach I'll pull down the branch for you.

Pietro noted how he never missed a chance to make himself agreeable but Ghisola, anticipating this too, smiled and said:

–There's no need.

But so haughtily Pietro started with surprise. He thought: *Why didn't I think of saying that to her? Now there's no time. How pleased she'd have been if I'd said it!*

All three stood together and gazed at one another in silence. For an instant they felt friends, no animosity. Also they felt a need to tell each other more than they'd done up to then.

Ghisola looked more cheerful. She flung back her hair and toyed with her apron-string, as if in invitation to make her undo it. But Pietro thought she wanted to go because he couldn't think of anything to say to her.

The base of the cherry-tree was black and dull red. Deep cracks had opened up in it, clefts filled with hard glossy resin. A file of ants swarmed up it, another alongside swarmed down: the tree seemed to feel them crawling over it. Nearby, where the turf was poached, lay a puddle of Bordeaux mixture. Over a strawberry-bed hung a fig-tree, completely leafless, quite smooth, its branches tangled together, its rind pink-white. Toads croaked from the bottom of the irrigation-trenches between the pollard red willows. There didn't seem to be any shadow but wisps of vapour, no higher than the vegetation, rose from where the soil had been dug.

Seeing Pietro absorbed Antonio nudged him. To prevent himself falling Pietro took a step forward that brought him next to Ghisola. He didn't utter a sound in case Antonio should pitch into him just there. It struck him she had a strong smell, a peculiar smell, it excited him. He thought too she'd made a move to open her arms to him. He was overwhelmed: *had she really?*

Antonio said to Ghisola:

– How can you mind about him? Don't you see how horrid he is?

Chiefly out of respect for the master's son she said it wasn't true but in a way Antonio wouldn't take too badly. Then she went on in defence of Pietro:

– What's it got to do with you?

With that Pietro was almost sure he wasn't the only one but he hadn't the strength to raise his eyes, though Antonio was stumped for an answer. Pietro looked at her and she smiled at him with one of those smiles involuntarily tender.

So Antonio, unable to think of anything better to stop the others staying together too long, said with all the venom he had:

– I'm going back to Siena.

Under her breath Ghisola whispered to Pietro but knowing all the same Antonio would hear:

– Let him go.

Then Antonio went off without waiting for Pietro but turning round angrily asked:

– Aren't you coming?

Ghisola said nothing and her silence gave nothing away but clearly she was putting Pietro to the test. With strangled voice he said to her:

– I've got to go. My father . . .

Her whole face hardened and she turned her eyes on Antonio, already several paces off.

Pietro begged her:

– Don't tell him anything.

She lowered her head and answered:

– Go then!

But Pietro believed he was loved. He caught Antonio up and put his arm through his. They began to snigger.

Meaning it but also to prevent Pietro thinking of Ghisola Antonio said:

– What did we come to Poggio a' Meli for? We didn't have any fun.

From an olive-tree a cicada chirruped. The millet rippled, first slow, then fast. Every so often a stalk seemed to shudder and shake open its light-coloured florets.

Antonio took a small knife with a fishtail handle of bone out of his pocket. Inserting the blade under the dried rind of a cane he'd picked up he sliced it off, nodal rings and all, with snicks that sounded like his sniggers.

Pietro didn't turn round to see where Ghisola was so Antonio shouldn't either. Antonio was pretending to be busy whittling. Actually he was eyeing Pietro on the sly but felt certain there was no need to.

When they got to the Porta Camollia they dusted their boots with their handkerchiefs, mopped the sweat off their faces and straightened their hats, each helping the other to reshape the dint in the middle.

Before entering the restaurant they promised each other neither would talk to Ghisola again.

Ghisola had resumed her walk to the fields with an exuberance that filled her whole being with joy, enhanced by the action of her legs. Her skirt and petticoat were so light she didn't feel them.

She mistrusted Antonio, who might blab to the master, and she took no account of Pietro. Best of the three she liked Agostino.

Just at that moment, running through the vine-rows and jumping across the spoor of young corn, he came towards her like when he'd been carrying a stake and smashed the pumpkins. He was in his shirt-sleeves, his arms plump and strong, veins proud in the firm flesh, and bareheaded. His green eyes glinting like ice looked lidless.

He jumped on her and threw her to the ground, making her cry. Teasing he asked:

– Hurt yourself?

– No! No!

Rising lightly to her feet she half-clasped him round the waist, to get him to do the same, but he pulled her arms down. She smiled, her face wet with tears. Wishing she could get away she pressed her feet close together. Sure of his strength the boy yelled into her ear:

– I'll do what I want with you. I'm not playing. You know that!

She dug her teeth into his arm. Pushing the arm forward Agostino bent her head back, forcing her teeth apart. In anger he asked:

– And what can you do now?

Ghisola spat and answered:

– I'm the weakest. Is that something for you to brag about? What a salty taste your skin's got!

He looked her in the eyes to intimidate her.

– When did you last see Pietro?

She put out the tip of her tongue.

– He doesn't come any more!

Recognizing him from indoors by his clothes he'd come out to meet him. He mimicked her voice:

– Really and truly?

– Not so far as I know!

– Did you think I was coming to pick cherries with him?

He pounced on her again, trying to tread on the toecaps of her boots, already out at the seams.

– Why didn't you tell me the truth? You can lie to the

others but not to me.

He went on forcing her backwards. But both of them fell down, hitting their heads together. That made him want to fight for real but he heard his mule's bells jingling:

– There's my brother coming back!

He raised himself on his knees the better to listen. Then he stood right up and went away singing out:

– He's overdriven her! . . . He's overdriven her! . . . He doesn't know how to handle her!

His sweaty cowlick flapped against his eyebrows. The ears being close-set his whole head, round at the back, looked like a ball.

Ghisola had stayed where she was, ashamed to find herself sprawling on the ground like that. She jumped up, brushed the dirt off and examined the ball of each thumb with the fist clenched, like in her rests from mowing.

When mowing she stuck the point of her sickle in the bole of a tree and adjusted her clothes, specially the blouse that was always coming undone, gripping between her teeth the hairpins she took out one at a time and re-set in her oily hair. After trying the sickle-point, wet with a sort of saliva from the torn wood, she began to sing, broke off and stood up straight. Then she spat in her hands and stooped again.

At times she had a desire to hold her face down and stay hidden, visible only from above, not eat any more and die without noticing it.

Also she had a desire to scream and felt afraid.

In the little time Anna spent at the farm and had no more to do indoors she had Ghisola draw water and fill the jugs. Then, with a watering-can, she watered the lemon-trees.

58

Evenings Giacco spudded up the grass that sprouted round the house, feeding it to the rabbits or the hens.

Anna went down to the vegetable patch and one of the women lifted lettuce and cut cabbage for her.

She'd have liked to grow flowers, if only because there was a garden near Poggio a' Meli she always went to see, hankering after one like it. But she had to make do with pinks and geraniums when given transplants. Even so she didn't dare grow many, as Domenico would be sure to ask was it for her health or to have a holiday she stayed in the country. Anyhow she was glad to have more than she had when she was a girl.

Even the few nicknacks she kept in her parlour in Siena had been so to speak compulsorily bought. There was a Jewish pedlar and whenever he couldn't pay his bill at the restaurant he brought all kinds of old things for her to look at, dumping them on the counter despite her objections. When he came back a week later it took Domenico and Anna half an hour to reach agreement and then, telling him this was the last time, settled for what they could. The pedlar swore he'd pay cash in future and they had a glass of wine together, as the shouting and abuse had made them hoarse.

But Anna was pleased and that's how she came to give house-room to the glass-paintings of *The five continents*, the yellowed alabaster flower-holders and the vases of genuine porcelain.

None of these was left in the parlour now. Instead an entire wall was covered with photographs of nearly everyone they knew and, standing on the top of a walnut-veneered whatnot, two plaster peasant women, leering. On the centre table stood a service of blue cut-glass, but imperfect, and round it five brass lamps with bow-knots permanently tied to the handles because they took them to church, with a flagon of oil, to be kept alight in Holy Week.

She cinnabared the floor-tiles at least once a month and

boots and shoes had to be quite clean before you came in.

When she was in the country and was brought flowers she wouldn't have them in the house but offered them to the Madonna of the monastery at Poggio al Vento. If it was too late and the chapel was shut she put them out in the open, on the porch table, and in the morning it was the first thing to be done.

To keep the sun off, because it always gave her a headache, she had a red ivory-handled parasol some years old. But when she saw the labourers' wives she felt ashamed and shut it, preferring to shelter under a tree. On the other hand she liked to take it to mass and on occasions even had Ghisola hold it up for her.

In church she sat a little apart from the local women who anyway left room for her of their own accord, out of respect.

She'd made herself a black dress trimmed at the collar with yellow silk and with a piece of lace falling from behind the shoulders as far as half-sleeves and attached to the belt. Over the trimming she wore a gold chain. While for the restaurant she had a red dress with blue and white bobbles.

She told Ghisola to learn to write, at least a little, but not trusting Pietro to teach her, because immediately he'd start pestering her, devoted an hour or two a day to it herself, when she felt better. It was Ghisola who made the ink out of wild mulberries. But she never got past the first pothooks.

To tell the truth Ghisola would have liked to learn: it impressed her greatly that Pietro went to school. At least she'd have liked to read, because lots of the girls she was friends with on the neighbouring farms had missals given them by the monks for their first communion. And then because in Piazza del Campo on Sunday mornings she longed to buy the printed songbooks on sale at a soldo each, with an account of some miraculous happening where there was always a Madonna with a big crown behind her head. The songs were nice too because they always had a picture before you came to the verses. She stopped with others in from the country to hear them being sung to the guitar by Cicciosodo, the ballad-singer who could move his top hat by wrinkling his forehead, standing on a stool. Then there were the monkeys that picked out numbers with Fortune's Wheel and a man who sold sweeties of different colours wrapped up in paper with fringes snipped out with the scissors.

When she got back to Poggio a' Meli she'd already learned the tune of the song she liked best but couldn't remember all the words. Sometimes, buying a copy after all and keeping it folded up in her pocket so Masa shouldn't see it, she had them read out to her by a friend when she met her in the fields. There were really lovely things in them, they moved her or made her laugh.

To keep Pietro occupied Anna put him to art school. He'd always had a bent for drawing and she and one or two of the customers considered it worth encouraging.

One morning at home, copying a bad engraved portrait, Pietro wondered why he had that yearning for Ghisola.

He stretched and twisted his neck to get a better look at the effect but in spite of his efforts the drawing was weak and inaccurate.

He was amazed he couldn't get it right. He curled his lip up and down till it touched the tip of his nose.

Old schoolbooks, soiled and coming to pieces, lay about his feet. Kicking against them produced a slight discomfort and this distracted him. The drawing irritated him too.

A familiar ache dashed his brain like a cold jet that never

let him get anything done. His very existence seemed strange to him. It made him afraid of himself and he tried to put himself out of his mind by fixing the palms of his hands in a long stare, till he succeeded in not seeing them any more.

Then he felt a crick at his left shoulder-blade. His whole being seemed to be reduced to it.

After a while he noticed the desk he was working at was too low and it was that had deadened his mind.

He stood up. The crayon fell and broke. He picked up the pieces with an acute and almost superstitious distaste: *why did it fall?*

He examined the portrait and then the copy, so disheartened he had to fight for breath, at the peak of the doubt and indecision that never left him in peace.

Meanwhile a sunbeam had soaked the whole of the sheet of paper in sleepy light. He thought: *That's it, I'm not going on.*

Rebecca, who'd been sweeping out the bedrooms, passed by and asked:

– Why are you sitting there doing nothing?

He leapt on her from behind, locking his hands across her face. Rebecca laughed, keeping her mouth shut and dribbling over his fingers. She staggered under his weight and he bounded into another room.

That same morning Ghisola took it into her head not to get up.

Masa asked crossly:

– Something the matter with you, sleepy-head?

Ghisola didn't answer and Masa went muttering into the kitchen to get her breakfast. After a while she opened the bedroom door again and standing in the doorway asked:

– Why don't you answer me? Are you playing me up this morning?

Ghisola gurgled and turned over under the bedclothes to face the wall.

Masa's anger was always short-lived and to put herself in the right she said:

– I saw you laughing!

She went on supping cold broth out of the bowl she was holding.

Ghisola was very tired, the kind of tiredness that at the time seems moral as well as physical.

But Masa went on with nerve-grating insistence:

– I've got no more breath to waste on you. And staying with you here I don't get anything done.

– Well don't stay then! Why can't I have some sleep? I don't want to work. Haven't I got to go back to Radda? Why are you such an old poker?

She felt she hadn't slept at all and was surprised Masa continued:

– And what if it's the master who won't have you here any more because you cheek me?

Masa made to hit her in the face with the spoon but licked it instead, both sides. At bottom she was fond of her and sorry they had to part. She went back to the kitchen.

Put in good humour by what Masa had said to her Ghisola got up. Still in her shimmy she made a chain of artificial flowers with wire twists used the year before for tying the grapes up. She hid it in her chest of drawers together with her snippets of coloured paper, soap-packets and a mass of ribbons and remnants. Sometimes she amused herself by stringing these out over the windowsill. There the pair of pigeons fluttered about, pecking on the panes to ask for maize or the dry breadcrumbs she always found in a corner of her apron pocket.

63

She made a point of not eating, though Masa had cut her a hunk of bread.

–What do you live on? Other times you guzzle.

Ghisola lifted the lid of the meal-chest and lowered her head inside to sniff the tang of yeast rising from the cross Masa had made with the back of a knife.

Then she went afield, singing at the top of her voice and thinking of her ribbons and scented soap-packets.

Where the grass was lush she stayed longest, where it was thin and short she gave it a quick swish with the sickle. From time to time she dried her hands, wiping off the dew on her skirt. The little tight-packed corn-cobs delighted her and she put the best ones on top to give to the calves herself. They gobbled them down like titbits, afterwards licking her hands and wrists, swinging their heads and jiggling the chains tied to their horns.

That champing in the silence of the byre! And how they drank out of the brim-full tubs! One gulp and the water-level sank at once! And last of all the sucking noises they made, rolling their tongues, taking deep breaths through their nostrils, their necks reaching up so high they had to open their mouths, moving away from the mangers sidelong.

This time she suddenly burst out crying and slamming the door with all her might ran to her granny's.

Ghisola wasn't well-behaved like she used to be. Wilful and headstrong she wanted to go her own way.

Every Sunday after dinner she sneaked out and wasn't seen again till dark. Granny went round the farms in search of her but she'd been mooching about Siena, in the streets, receiving obscene compliments and propositions. One or two of the fellows recognized her and followed to stop and talk. She smiled, flattered and rather bewildered, cause they weren't country lads, they were smart young work-men. When she arrived at the Porta Camollia she had to be sharp because the toll-booth guards would mill round and block her way through.

And when she was wearing a flower she hadn't to walk against the wall as some of the shopmen standing at their doors would stretch out their hands to snatch it.

When she came home she escaped grumbles by getting in through the bedroom window, clinging to the supports of the hen-house. She undressed and got into bed sup-perless, maddened by the clatter Giacco and Masa made dipping their brass spoons in the tureen. Whenever these clashed Giacco caught Masa's eye.

In the end granny realized she was in and thinking she'd been taken unwell brought her a piece of bread on the sly but before giving it to her boxed her ears with it.

Ghisola chewed, her head turned to the wall, astonished the bread was wet with tears that wouldn't stop: just before she'd felt more like laughing. Was this to be her life?

But hearing her grandparents come in she shut her eyes, to make them think she was asleep and out of a need not to see them.

On her last night at Poggio a' Meli, as she was going to sleep, holding in her mouth a hairpin she'd been nibbling, she seemed to fall from a great height bang on the roof of the house at Radda. She groaned and shook all over. From the other bed her grandfather called out:

– Keep quiet! Do you think I like it either?

She was afraid she'd get scolded. She thought it over and seemed to hear a voice saying out loud: *They're not bothering now. Only you mustn't snore.*

But the smell of the unwashed sheets turned her off and so as not to smell it she folded them down at her neck.

Her hair was undone and ending in a point looked on the bolster like a scythe.

65

She dreamt she was coming home: Mum had a new dress, her two sisters had put on fat. A voice asked:

– What are you doing here?

She answered:

– I don't know. I didn't come of my own accord. But where's Daddy got to?

– It's all your fault.

It was the voice again.

Her mother and sisters were listening and looking on, in a silence so horrible she rushed at them to make them go into the next room. But in her dream she couldn't move her arms and her head hit an invisible wall. She felt her heart was changing position, it was the same with her tummy, and her throat was peeling. Her mother's face and her sisters' faces grew terrifying. She cried out:

– Speak to me!

They turned towards a door. Upstairs came Dad with two bulging sacks on his back, his face dripping blood, blood enough to fill the millpond.

Feeling the weight of the sacks upon her she howled.

Pietro liked wild flowers best, the wishy-washy blooms with scents that are indistinct and almost alike. Garden flowers he never thought of without blushing and getting flustered. It was his habit to fill his pockets with daisies, red ones and white ones, yellow dandelions, white and pink vetch, corn-poppies, broom, violets, dog-roses, may, wild pea-blossom. Then he'd mumble the stalks.

Ghisola had taught him how you can make ink from mulberries and get a thin honey taste by sucking some reddish flowers looking like the wild lilies that grow in the corn but not so tall, and when red berries in the hedgerows are ripe to eat. She'd taught him to stop him throwing clods at her when he caught her hopping from one baulk to another, probably not to work.

One day while having lunch he heard Ghisola had gone back to Radda. Rebecca was telling Adamo. He lifted his head to hear better and went on eating but sat hunched at the foot of the table till evening, his head gripped in his fists.

Rain began to sluice the window-panes as if it meant to flood the room. It was one of those driving rains that beat against a wall as though to knock it down but all of a sudden fall straight, bright and transparent. Then you see them turned the other way. Then they vanish, till from time to time a droplet pricks you in the face like an ice-cold needle. The streets change hue, draw breath, fill with sun that turns to shade and then to light again, while from the Montagnola, as if breaking cover, clouds come straight for Siena, passing over Monte Amiata.

Streets that go in every direction, brushing against one another, drawing apart, joining together again, two or three times, stopping as if not knowing where to go next, with little lopsided squares, steep-sloping, deep-sunken, hemmed in by the ancient mansions.

Houses in lines curved or twisted, getting mixed up, as if each street was trying to go its own way, with bits of the countryside glimpsed through the crack of an alley seen at an angle, from the steps of a church or from some forgotten and deserted arcade.

Pietro fancied they were spiting Ghisola by making her walk all on her own, sopping wet. Turning such things in his mind over and over, he fell asleep.

He'd already wasted a year of his time at art school with his future still unsettled, the question depending on the various opinions of the oldest customers and on his father, who rarely remembered it and when he did lost his temper. Anna persevered however, even after that unsuccessful test of draughtsmanship, being convinced he was intelligent. But she was fated not to be able to do anything for him.

One morning she decided to take him to the priest and ask his advice. She'd already prepared her best clothes and was making haste so her husband shouldn't get to know, the visit was sort of secret. All of a sudden she felt her heart tighten, tighter and tighter, but she couldn't cry out. She wasn't even aware she fell.

She was found lying with her head on the floor-tiles, by the wardrobe she'd opened, stretched out full length, the way animals go that are struck on the back of the head with the edge of the heel, her eyes only half-shut and still bright, her face slightly contracted, as if it was only for the sake of others she minded dying and begged not to be scolded for it, with an indescribable expression of painful concern.

The first one to see her was Rebecca, she'd come looking to do her hair. At once she uncorked the bottles of medicine kept for when it was a convulsion, but Anna had stopped breathing.

– Mistress! Mistress!

Terrified and all of a tremble she ran to the kitchen and shouted from the window that looked onto the restaurant door. A waiter caught the words:

– The master! Tell him to come quick!

Thinking it an attack of convulsions more severe than usual the waiter put down the cloth he was holding and went into the kitchen:

– Where's the boss?

– Not back yet. He stayed to pay the chemist.

– Run and fetch him. The mistress is ill.

The kitchen-help who'd answered put down the knife

he'd been using to gut the fish heaped in the sink and only just taken out of the basket, dried his hands, tucked his apron up to the waist-band and set out. But he couldn't find Domenico immediately, he'd gone to do some more marketing.

When he found him the two came back at a trot. On the stairs Domenico collided with the doctor, a friend as well as a customer, coming down to wait for him.

– My dear Domenico . . . Listen to me a moment!

He took the doctor by the shoulders. The doctor removed his hands, keeping hold of his wrists.

– Domenico, this time . . . Poor woman! . . .

He shouted:

– Let me go! It's a convulsion!

But he felt himself freeze through and through, with a freezing that came in waves from his fingertips and stopped in the middle of his head. For a moment he thought his mind disturbed but his laboured breathing, he who breathed so freely, reminded him something he'd foreboded had come about. How could he face it? How see Anna dead? Did he have to go himself?

When he went into the bedroom the walls and doors lurched and gaped and he didn't seem to see anything. Then he touched the face, already cold and slightly rigid. He shut his eyes, slumped across his wife and began to bawl.

His mere bellowing made him tremble.

Little by little he felt his grief. All his tremendous violence now seemed turned to fearfulness. He thought Poggio a' Meli was being dragged far away, leaving him no time to do anything, the doors of his restaurant were closing of themselves and wouldn't reopen, Anna had suffered so much through not being able to say anything. Everything in him crumbled.

His grief was so great everybody would have to console him! Now he was sorry he hadn't loved her enough!

Anna had gradually turned cold and when someone

closed her eyes looked to those round her for the first time strangely unfamiliar.

One took her by the chin and keened:

– Who knows what she would have said? How she suffered! Poor woman! So good!

When Pietro saw her she'd already been laid on the bed. He didn't know what to think. Domenico only spoke to him when reminded to. But without any affection, as if under a compulsion to avoid him. And now more than ever hoping to keep him at home, for the sake of the restaurant. Meanwhile he went on crying loud enough to be heard in the street.

– She looks as if she was just going to get down off the bed!

Said Rebecca.

All at once Domenico went to her again, touched her hair, made a desperate gesture and howled louder. Feeling nothing beyond a vague unease Pietro leant on the pillows and tried to shed tears. Within himself he wondered if everybody else felt as little as he did and he had a vague sense of relief when his father was far enough away for him not to see or hear his sorrowing, as repugnant to him as his anger.

Rebecca said to him:

– Poor mummy, she loved you so much!

It meant little to him, or to be exact he took exception to the remark and went away to find something to do, ashamed of himself.

The morning of the funeral he'd forgotten all about it when he caught sight through the half-open door of his father approaching. He had a fear, he couldn't tell why, he was going to be beaten till the blood ran.

Domenico said:

– Get dressed. They'll be coming soon to take your poor mother away.

Pietro forced himself to obey. Or rather he was now terrified some calamity was going to happen to him!

70

He got out of bed and while dressing acted to himself, trying to imitate gestures of grief he had observed.

So that he ended up feeling speechless merriment mixed with terror.

But when they made him kiss his mother before placing her in the coffin, he thought: *Why don't I get in too? Put me in.*

Then he had an extraordinary fright: *You think she's dead? You're all pretending. It's just another make-believe. I knew she'd do something horrid to hurt me and I don't deserve it.*

He sobbed, overwhelmed by dark despair. Why hadn't they told him before that she was dead?

He stayed with those who'd coffined the corpse but wouldn't even touch the hem of the shroud. He was astonished the others did everything as though it was an ordinary job of work, with tears and the apparently interminable marks of affection: straightening the head on the special pillow with the embroidered monogram, putting the feet together, settling on the hair a flower that had slipped between the shoulder and the coffin.

He would have liked nobody to be there: all those hands made him ill. Those hands, those hands!

He wanted to cry out: *Take her away quickly. Why haven't you taken her away? I don't want her in the house any more!* He wondered his father didn't lose his temper but all the attentions had calmed him a little.

At his own wish Pietro followed the hearse to the cemetery in a closed carriage, tugging at the old blinds of blue silk so that no one should see him. Domenico would have preferred to go on foot, saving money as well. But Pietro's main concern was the people stopping in the street, right in front of the house-door, to gawk. He noticed they raised themselves on their toes and craned their necks to have a better view.

Anna's death was a real setback for Domenico. His employees began to slack and depression made him furious, quicker-tempered: more often than not he'd blame someone for something entirely without cause. He became tighter-fisted too and many of the plans for the farm and the restaurant had to be dropped. He had more work to do and he couldn't withstand fatigue. And he was quite incapable of taking the interest he should have taken in his son. On the whole he left him to his own devices but sometimes, when he thought better of that, treated him inconsiderately and with such undue violence even Rebecca went to his defence. Then he desisted but at the next opportunity did worse, as if he'd got to justify himself.

Anna had died in the second week of January and every Sunday, before daybreak, Domenico visited her grave with two bunches of flowers. He'd wanted to carry one himself and give one to Pietro but Pietro wouldn't have it. Bending at the knees under the blows, bitterly humiliated, he said:

– But why? You oughtn't to kick me.

Suppose someone had recognized him?

In the sky were beginning those immense glimmers that come from the still distant dawn. The streets were gloomy and damp.

Usually there were only a few passers-by. They walked fast and everything they said rang clear, their voices like their clouted boots re-echoing on the cobbles. A few, mostly porters on their way to meet trains, lit pipes, covering the match with both hands.

When they were nearly halfway there Domenico stopped

at a café where a girl was in a dress so low-cut Pietro was afraid it would open right out.

She smiled at her clients and then her firm round powdered cheeks swelled till they narrowed her eyes. She doled out that smile as she doled out the little gold-rimmed china cups.

Pietro wouldn't go in. Domenico came out again and dragged him inside.

The girl coquetted with Domenico but Pietro stood aside hanging his head, caught in the trammels of the girl and the girl's ways and the wall-length mirrors, not even knowing how to drink his coffee. He burned his fingers and scalded his mouth.

He came out before his father had finished drinking his and through the windows misted with steam condensing into long winding rills saw him having laughs with the girl.

A purer light lit the tower of the Palazzo Pubblico and the cloudless sky swarmed with swallows squealing, each of their squeals the length of an arc of their flight. The Piazza del Campo was rose-coloured with a few strips of green grass and the stumpy columns of white stone.

– Next Sunday I'll go in without him making me.

But this kind of timidity seemed to increase week by week. It got like an illness and at the thought of it he felt his forehead bathed in cold sweat. Afterwards his hands stiffened in his pockets, the lining caught in his fingers and his feet refused to move.

Anyhow Domenico walked slowly too and when he had a cold stopped to take his handkerchief out and blow his nose.

Going up the Via di Città and then the Via Stalloreggi Pietro was always more sad.

On reaching the cemetery Domenico chatted with Braciola, the gravedigger the colour of his earth, fat as if crawling with worms and with side-whiskers nearly white. Standing the flowers in two long china containers, a little water at the bottom, almost black, never changed, he'd look round and exclaim:

– How fast it's spreading! When your mother died the graves only came up to here.

He stayed looking and then asked:

- The widow hasn't been this morning?

– Before we got here perhaps. Let's go, it's no use waiting for her.

– It's early yet. Why don't you want to wait for her? She brings flowers every morning.

He found fault with his son for having no regard for the only other visitor in the cemetery at that time of day!

But the widow was beginning to feel her devoted loyalty was losing point. Why should Rosi of all people adopt the same habit when the whole of Siena knew he hadn't adored his wife as much as he now tried to make out?

She'd cast him a mistrustful glance and return his greeting with constraint. And what an impression the boy made on her! Not even looking at the graves, his hands in his pockets and his manner half-asleep or impertinent!

Pietro broke out:

– I'm going.

This bickering got worse each time. Once, towards the end of winter, Domenico ordered him:

– Be off with you.

Pietro flushed but said:

– What's she to me?

Dew had given the earth on the fresh graves a kneaded look. A few birds flew across, tilted to one side. In between the cypresses the mountains looked like long streaks of paint still wet.

The headstones were covered with small grey snails. The Cathedral became whiter and whiter and, gazing at it, Pietro realized he was choking with anger.

They met the widow at the entrance gate and Domenico wished her good morning. She answered without turning

74

her head but squinnying at Pietro. Domenico stopped and said, as he did every time:

– She's going to her husband's grave.

Nobody knew her except by sight and Domenico had no more information about her than anyone else had. On her return from the cemetery, where she prayed at least half an hour, she went shopping and no one saw her again till the morning after.

She was short and fat and as she walked along her bosom bounced as though rebounded from the protuberant stomach. Her tiny hat was held on by a length of elastic going round her ears and under her throat. At every step she took an old grey-green feather on it shook as if flicked. Through her thin hair pinned up tight the nape of her neck showed greasy and pink as goose-skin. She always dressed the same way and had for heaven knows how long, not perhaps out of poverty.

After watching her go Domenico asked his son:

– What are you thinking about?

Pietro smiled and said:

– Me? Nothing.

– Then why are you holding your head down?

– I didn't know I was. You know I didn't.

– It makes you look nasty, not nice, the way I got you. And why do you want to go back to school? Didn't you get yourself expelled?

Domenico mentioned school resentfully and at the times he thought Pietro most suggestible.

Pietro remained silent, feeling faint. His father would never miss a chance to taunt him with that, turn it to his advantage!

Observing his confusion and mortification Domenico went on:

– You could give me a hand and in a few years' time get married.

It would suit Domenico to marry him off soon, now

75

there was no one to take charge in the restaurant. Several times he'd given him a quizzical look, sizing him up, checking it wasn't too early, though Pietro was only sixteen.

– I . . . shan't get married.

– In that case I'll have to marry again. Think on it. Would you mind?

Pietro hesitated but not to be put off from further schooling answered:

– Who would it be?

To test his real feelings his father answered:

– I'll tell you presently.

He looked at him. But Pietro had been quite unconcerned. He added:

– They told me . . . that lady . . . who's got two daughters. The lady . . . who came for a meal the day before yesterday.

It was just a rumour. Domenico took him up.

– You'd better marry one of them.

– Me?

He blushed again because it seemed something far above him, though it unsettled him slightly.

– I'll tell you which one I'd like you to have.

He laughed:

– I know. The young one.

But Domenico didn't answer. He was already thinking he'd forgotten the evening before to send word to the labourers to take the cows to be serviced.

– If you don't answer why did we mention it?

Pietro dared to ask. But Domenico shouted angrily:

– You're not fit to meddle in what I do. Expect me to feed your wife as well? So stop it! Look: you'd better go to Poggio a' Meli!

He drew from his waistcoat fob, as he did at every opportunity, a small black rosary he kept there together with a few gold sovereigns. Nearly touching Pietro's forehead with the cross he uttered his usual commonplace:

– See this? It's to remind me of my poor mother Gigella. I carried it round everywhere with me. That's all she gave me when I left home to come to Siena. What have you got to remind you of your mother?

But noting in his turn Pietro wasn't even listening he became anxious. It seemed impossible a son should carry on like that! To think he'd even intended naming him after himself! He was to be so like him, belong to him!

He could have taken hold of him and snapped him in two like a twig! That his own son should elude his control! Shouldn't he be more biddable, not less?

All at once there dawned on him an insidious suspicion that his son too was another person like anybody else.

Then he'd better not have been born. Why had he had him? Best not talk to him any more, put up with him walking alongside in silence, his head held so low it might hit the pavement.

Pietro took the keys to the restaurant staff waiting in the street and went in with them but, not wanting to stay as he was supposed to, popped back to the house. Domenico had handed him the keys without meeting his eye and when he finished his marketing had him sent for. He'd left the staff unsupervised.

– You'll never make a boss. How can you give orders if you don't learn yourself?

He now spoke to his son to relieve his feelings and his reproof was kindly. Taking up the bunches of birds to be spit-roasted he said:

– This is a thrush, this is a lark. Help me pluck them.

He seated himself before a skep the feathers went into. Pietro was wool-gathering, he hummed a little to himself and then answered:

– If you don't mind I'll go and read a book.

Domenico finished spitting the birds he'd plucked, adjusted the jack and then asked:

– What book is it?

– When I tell you you still won't understand.

Raising one hand on high Domenico pronounced in his authoritarian manner:

– I understand more than all the scholars do because I'm your father. No one knows what you need better than I do.

He laid his hand upon his chest, as if affirming truth: on his blood-stained and feather-bestuck apron. Then he went to the stove, broke up the chunky charcoal with the shovel, took Tiburzi by the shoulders and bent him down to the stokehole, shouting:

– Can't you see for yourself it's burning better?

Domenico had stopped thinking about Pietro but seeing him still there dashed at him with fist clenched:

– Be off with you!

Pietro stayed where he was and lowered his head, looking up from underneath.

Not even the breathless activity of the cooks, constantly urged on, sworn at and pushed about, for Domenico always wanted dishes prepared in an hour, could rouse him from those daydreams.

Domenico's fury had reduced everybody to silence: no one could help doing what he said, even if it meant making things worse. But when he went into a dark corner to hang some cuts he wanted left uncooked, Guerrino suddenly turned to Pietro, putting his tongue out to remind him of one of the funny stories he'd told him the evening before. They all grinned, without stopping their work. Pietro whispered:

– Tell me another.

Slithering on a slice of bacon-rind the cook signalled to him to wait. Tiburzi, his blue jacket puckered and bulging

over the apron-string, kept watch, turning his eyes without moving his head, stomping his feet in merriment and
keeping his arms in the warm water of the greasy tubs
filled with plates to wash up. He had a goitre, hard and
yellowy, as if it had got a stone in it, like a plump pullet's
crop.

But Domenico often pretended to see and hear nothing,
it was a way of getting to know his employees, and he
came back saying:

– So Ghisola led you into bad ways too!

Alarmed and taken by surprise Pietro asked:

– Why?

Everyone turned in his direction, sprightly inquisitive.

How could he put the blame on her? Some one must
have been telling him tales! So that was why he'd sent her
back to Radda! It made him sympathize with her, resent
the unjust jibes at her expense and want to see her again.
But why was everyone looking at him slyly, chuckling
with amusement? And what made his father so certain?
He sat with his fingertips propped on the desk, in misery.

He was now a thin pale youth with a trick of holding
one shoulder higher than the other. He dressed badly, with
a red string-tie round a collar always rumpled and dirty:
fair hair, ears too big and sticking out from the sides of
his head, eyes of the clearest blue and with a look in
them as though there was something he had to defend.
His face wore a set expression, ingenuous and melancholy
but assured and resolute, tending towards the truculent and
the disagreeable.

Sometimes for days on end he looked unhappy but if
anyone spoke to him he became calm and affable. He didn't
stammer so much.

The impact things made on him remained undefined and
that fretted him. Springtime was like an act of violence.
Reading a book under a tree in spring! He'd break off in
mid-page, at random, to stand up and draw a branch down
to his face, as though to be caressed. He'd have liked to

ask its consent, seeing before him hill-slopes clothed with gleaming luxuriant foliage, here and there almonds and peaches hanging as if ready to strew themselves on the ground. Making sure nobody had noticed him he sighed and resumed his reading. He hadn't yet found the book for his soul. Sometimes he left off reading because he seemed to be seeing through the pages, the leaves becoming flimsy or getting holes in them.

If an insect crawled up his trousers and onto the book, he stopped then too.

An occasional bird darted amidst the blossoms with the force and action of a needle and thread, as though the leaves had opened up for it and then closed round again.

Even before Anna died he wouldn't go to church and she hardly ever succeeded in making him say his prayers. He now considered himself an atheist. To reject the prejudices of the priests he used swear-words. Domenico put it down to those damned schoolbooks.

Domenico always had the animals at Poggio a' Meli castrated. The labourers joked about it, with double meanings Giacco and Masa thought aimed at their granddaughter.

– That's good. Now they won't leave home and they'll plump up better.

Sometimes there were a dozen cockerels caponised, subdued, pecking reluctantly, their feathers spattered with blood. In the byre the calves stunned, dejected, their eyes darker and gloomier.

The dog stretched out on the threshing-floor, the cats silent and spiteful, cowering under the waggon or behind the woodstack, their eyes ever open.

This time from a litter of kittens he picked out one tom

to keep at the restaurant. The gelder took hold of it, held it head down in a sack nipped between his knees and made a cut with a jack-knife. At first the kitten was going to stay in the sack, drained of its strength, then it mewed and jumped out, disappearing somewhere.

– That's it. He nearly forgot to miaow!

– Well that didn't take long!

They laughed in admiration.

Holding himself somewhat aloof, to enhance the disgust, Domenico said:

– What do I owe you?

– One lira. Is that too much?

– One lira?

– Oh give me what you like. You always get your own way anyhow.

A stroke had skewed his mouth and his bleary eyes watered without stop.

– I'll give you half a lira and you can come and have a plate of spaghetti at the restaurant.

He counted out the coins.

The man hefted them a moment in his palm. Then, with an expression of malicious discontent, he dropped them in his pocket, first looking to see it wasn't torn.

– As long as there's plenty of spaghetti!

Casting his eyes round the labourers gathered for lunch he poked Domenico in the paunch and said:

– See how fat the rich get!

But the labourers pretended not to hear and Carlo put a hand to his lips. Pietro asked:

– I wonder where the kitten went. Shall I go and look?

– Let him be. He'll come back when he's hungry.

– He won't die?

He asked the gelder.

– Not a chance. They lick the wound till it heals up. They're better at doctoring themselves than we are!

They talked about the other animals he'd castrated, Spot in particular, who put his tail between his legs and snarled when other dogs approached. Everybody looked in his direction and he slunk off as if he'd understood. But he soon came back because the labourers were having lunch, chatting from the open doors that faced each other across the yard, while the women finished their housework.

– Draw me a jug of water, Adele! said Carlo, advancing from his place.

She did so and left the jug on the well-curb, while the spring-hook of the well-chain went on swinging.

The men had kept her under their eyes. Then one by one they drank and sopped their slices of dry bread.

Moving about the yard they exchanged opinions on the field-work while waiting for the return of the master, he'd gone to see the cows.

Standing among them Pietro took interest in seeing how they chewed. Some, so as not to waste the crumbs, threw their heads back and tipped the bread into their mouths from the hollow of their hands.

Carlo was a big man, though in winter he got leg pains. His calico shirt was always the cleanest. But he stank of dung and his breath reeked of the garlic and onions he was such a glutton for. At each bite he took he looked at the tooth-prints on his bread.

Considering him of more consequence than the others the gelder shook his coins up and showed him them before leaving:

– See? They're like us, some one sort, some another. This one's had a hammering and you can hardly tell what it is. This one's bent, like one of us who's crippled, and this one they've tried to make a hole in, like when you knife somebody or they knife you, and this one's so worn down it only weighs half as much. It's poor like I am and I'll drink it up first so it won't make me think about it. So long.

He spat and swore.

Carlo hardly answered. When he was out of earshot he said:

82

– He wanted to lunch on my bread. But it didn't come off.

He glanced towards his quarters, where the meal-chest still stood open.

Three years had passed. Pietro had got his certificate of education. Re-entered at the technical school he had in fact, after a lot of difficulty and not a little self-distrust, buckled down to his bookwork.

He spent his free time with fellow-students. Domenico even let them come inside the restaurant to pick him up.

That was when he began frequenting women. He went in secret, obtaining the money by selling books or some article he contrived to convey out of the house without Domenico noticing: a majolica service, some gemstone medallions, one time an antique fan made of ivory and silk. He replaced the keys under a woollen mat used to stand a lamp on.

One of Domenico's casuals at Poggio a' Meli fell in love with Rebecca and let it be known he'd be willing to marry her. For some time Domenico had had another niece of Rebecca's staying on the farm, a cousin of Ghisola's also from Radda. So he felt able to give his consent, making the niece take the place of her aunt. It was he provided the dowry and met many other expenses too, taking the husband on as a waiter into the bargain.

Following Anna's death Rebecca had remained on good terms with Domenico but this niece, Rosaura, took her place very soon after and up to the wedding aunt and niece quarrelled, in the restaurant too, to the great alarm of Giacco and Masa, who had no wish to jeopardize the bread of their old age.

Masa kept out of sight so as not to be seen always having a sit-down. She was afraid she'd get the sack, all the more as even she didn't altogether trust the master, knowing him better than the others did. Seating herself she'd lift her skirt up, roll down her white cotton stockings and scratch her legs, where she felt continual pain.

The other women came to know of it and as they got the same wages held it against her, calling her a scrounger, but still helped her with her work so as to stay in her good books.

As a matter of fact the reason why Domenico continued to indulge her was she kept him informed about all that went on at the farm.

But Giacco had given up asking Pietro for cigar-butts. Thinking he'd turned out bad he went so far as to lay complaints against him, telling Domenico that but for himself, a poor old man everybody looked down on, they'd have walked off with the bricks of the Poggio a' Meli threshing-floor in collusion with his son.

– He's got no sense! If you don't mind me saying so . . . Begging your pardon . . . Why blame it on me?

Domenico reassured him vaguely but on purpose not completely. Then Giacco acted aggrieved and to make out he'd spoken reluctantly clammed up.

Sometimes, taking his hat off and brushing it against his knees, he'd whimper, alluding to Pietro:

– Some people are born lucky!

He didn't work with the other men any more, only did his granddaughter's old jobs. He'd grown knock-kneed and his legs looked shorter, like two bellropes sometimes do if they twine together.

When he had something to say his big head made an effort to sit straight on his narrow rounded shoulders. He had a nondescript face, the skin withered into wrinkles like little sun-tanned strops between which grime collected. His mouth was hidden under a ruffled moustache that looked like animal hair. The conjunctivae of his eyes had yellowed and thickened.

Before addressing any task he'd scratch behind his ears with one hand, holding his hat aloft in the other, as if trying to think it out.

When the young master went by he'd tweak his sleeve and ask:

– Don't you talk to me any more?

It was true Pietro did shun him. He disliked his two-faced ways, ruthless self-interest appeared through a show of respect.

Holding him back Giacco would say with a diffidence he tried to make sound affectionate:

– Yet I've known you since you were a little boy and dandled you on my knee. Maybe you're cross with me?

He tried to make Pietro smile so as not to have to acknowledge he'd wasted his words. Darkly, persuasively, resentfully he went on:

– Why don't you like me?

Pietro didn't know what to answer but was pleased to see him grovel.

– Yet I've always done my duty. Your father knows that. And I'll go on doing it so long as God gives me strength.

With this his voice took on an arrogant note.

Pietro had an aversion to this insistency, certainly put on.

The old man held him with his eye. Pietro gave him a timid glance and unloosed his sleeve.

Giacco tried to smile but seeing the expression on Pietro's face couldn't bring himself to it. But Pietro felt released, and not only because he could go now.

Once he asked him:

– How's Ghisola?

Giacco perked up, sensing the way he might win favour with the young master but hesitating to use it:

– It's a long time since you mentioned her!

– But where is she?

Instead of telling him at once, giving too much away, Giacco scratched his chest. A rent in his shirt showed nipples black-blooded with long hairs and enlarged pores. An old sweat-stained satchet of medallions hung from a cotton thread that cut a groove round his neck.

– She's at Radda I think.

He spoke quietly and pointed with his sickle to the Chianti hills.

– She wrote two months ago . . . Do you see? Radda's over there.

– Have you still got the letter?

– My wife had it. I think she kept it. Think so anyway. Hang it, she won't have thrown it away!

Implying she had.

Pietro asked:

– Why thrown it away? If you're fond of her you must still have it. I want to see it.

He spoke as though demanding a right. His hostility to the old man sharpened. Undecided what to say but eager to know more Giacco went on:

– She sent something else as well.

He winked.

– What? Her photo I expect?

Laying a hand on his shoulder and withdrawing it quickly Giacco asked:

– Who told you?

– Didn't she send her photograph? Tell.

Leaning against an olive-tree to continue Giacco exclaimed jauntily;

– Yes she did!

He was like a tortoise that starts moving again when sure it's not going to be molested any more.

Pietro turned about and without saying anything else went to where the old man lived. He felt an immense happiness. Radda seemed only a few kilometres away!

The ears of corn, bent under wind and rain, hook-shaped, were thinly gilded, the stalks tangled, some broken.

Giacco called after him:

– Listen to me, listen to me . . .

Masa was sitting on the bedroom doorsill, drying plates.

– Your husband has told me you've got a letter from Ghisola. Have you?

Masa had often thought of letting him read it and she answered truthfully, then asked:

– He told you?

– Didn't you want him to?

Not waiting for her to stand up he entered the bedroom, stepping over her as she lowered her back.

He liked Masa better but in talk with the master she ran him down as much as Giacco did.

– I'm coming! Stop rummaging in the drawers . . . You won't find it.

He was annoyed but only said:

– Hurry up then. You're so dense. You don't know how much I think of her.

He was afraid Giacco would come in. With him there he'd keep quiet, the looks Giacco sometimes shot him made him unsure of himself, if not wary.

Masa found the letter but before giving it to him held it in her open hand against her sunken chest:

– I don't want the master to know anything about this.

– Why? Who's going to tell him?

She flushed and answered:

– You know why better than I do.

She pursed her lips like she did when nibbling cotton to thread a needle.

The envelope, as he saw with displeasure, had been pinched open, torn all round between finger and thumb, to take out the letter Ghisola must have dictated to one of her relations as she didn't know how to write. Pietro read it all, out loud: her parents had had the measles, aunty Giuseppina couldn't feed her baby herself.

Then he asked:

– And the photograph, where is it?

Masa laughed, his presumptuousness pleased her. Again and again she dug her knuckles into her sides. When she laughed her teeth showed close-set and still white.

– It fell down behind the chest of drawers a week ago. When I was going to dust it.

Under a line of holy pictures hanging from a short piece of string along the wall he did in fact see an old blue velvet frame, empty. That emptiness, a sheet of blank paper in it, brought a lump to his throat.

– And you haven't bothered to pick it up?

Now he felt sure he'd see it.

Masa wasn't having any rebukes and she said:

– All in good time. Who cares? In the morning we get up early and in the evening we don't feel like doing it because we're tired out.

– I'll move the chest.

When there was respect to be shown he worked too!

– Don't. It'll worry me.

But her eyes weren't spiteful like other times. There was tenderness in them though clouded and doubtful.

– Why?

– It's heavy and you might hurt yourself. Then I'd get the blame from the master.

When she mentioned his father Pietro felt he had to assert himself somehow.

– Well help me then!

They were close to wrangling but without hurry, one at a time, she removed all the ornaments: a chipped china vase with ever so many flowers in it, a wax image of Saint Catherine under a bell-jar, a fragment of looking-glass fly-blown and verdigrised.

– Be patient.

He dragged the wormholed chest towards him and the

88

photograph, caught between it and the wall, dropped down. He picked it up and without taking his eyes off it went to the window, with the same fear as when lightning has struck close by.

– See how beautiful she is now! Now you'd really like her!

Instantly Pietro understood what beautiful meant. His heart-beats quickened with happiness. Feeling his lips quiver he didn't reply.

Masa kept her eyes fixed on him, unsure what he'd do or how he was taking it: his eyelids were fluttering. She nudged his arm and asked:

– And what shall we do with it now?

She was afraid he'd want to take it away. But Pietro wouldn't have dared, Ghisola might object. He answered in a strained voice:

– Keep it here, in its frame. Do as I say. Don't let it fall down again.

Satisfied, Masa consented and wiped the cobwebs off the wall with a rag. Pietro himself replaced the photograph in its frame and realigned the chest of drawers against the wall.

– Keep the letter too.

– To tell the truth, if she'd behaved better towards us . . . I'd be more fond of her.

At an abrupt gesture of Pietro's, unlike any she'd seen him make before, she went on:

– But I love her just the same.

– What harm did she do to you? I'd like to know what harm she may have done you! You're making it up!

– I can't discuss it. It's my business. Nobody else's.

She'd taken offence she'd had to send her granddaughter away! She bit her bottom lip, rapidly and repeatedly.

– Keep this to yourself. Don't tell anybody I've shown it to you, not even Rebecca. Go away now and woe betide you if you let anybody as much as suspect!

He went out. All at once he realized he was in love with

Ghisola. He found nothing unexpected or unpleasant about it, on the contrary if he'd been more sure of her he'd have told Masa there and then. Explaining it was above all a matter of social reparation, a task he'd gladly devote himself to. Why shouldn't Ghisola be well off too?

Three days later he returned to Poggio a' Meli.

On the sunlit barn lay the shadow of a pear-tree, weightless and motionless. But those lines of shadow seemed to him like signs of fever, throbbing like his veins, like water on the boil.

On the top of the linhay, and all of it visible because the roof sloped to a metre off the ground, the houseleek had grown two metres across, one plant almost growing into the other, with spiky leaves and a flower the stalk hadn't strength to hold up. There too were the straw casing of a wine-flask and two rusty scythes. And there, so it should get the sun, Carlo kept between two stones a medicine bottle full of oil, with a scorpion in it, using it to treat cuts.

On the highest part of the roof Pietro noticed a remnant of cloth now sun-faded, stuck there by the rain: a half-slip of Ghisola's.

He went to Masa's and said to her:

– Let me see the photo again.

He took a quick look at it where it hung on the wall, in case Masa should take offence and perhaps write and tell her granddaughter.

Monte Amiata had a liquid appearance and seemed about to be settling down.

Slightly built and frequently ill, Pietro had always incurred Domenico's dislike. Now he was thin and pale Domenico considered him incompetent: just another nincompoop!

He felt his slender neck, running a finger along the veins, smooth and all too easy to see. Pietro lowered his eyes, thinking he had to apologize for it as for something he'd done wrong. Such docility evaded Domenico's violence but made him more irritable. He was impelled to torment him.

Those books! He could have crushed them under his heel! Catching sight of Pietro carrying them he sometimes couldn't restrain himself and knocked them into his face.

A book-writer was a swindler, he wouldn't give one of them a meal on tick!

Meanwhile Pietro had involved him in fees for the technical school three years running!

After a long look at his ear or the weak concave back of his neck he'd make savage gestures, bite his lip, plonk his knife on the table and stop eating.

Pietro was silent and uncomplaining but not obedient. He stayed in as little as possible and when he needed money for school waited till one of the more important customers was about: when any of those were there Domenico didn't refuse. He'd found out how to resist by bearing it all without a murmur. School he came to consider chiefly an excuse for keeping away from the restaurant.

Meeting sarcastic hostility in his father's eye he didn't even try asking him for a little affection.

But how could he get away from him? It needed only a glance less fearful than usual for Domenico to place his hand over Pietro's face, that hand that could lift a barrel. And sometimes when Pietro had trembled and smiled, saying: *One day I'll be as strong as you are*, Domenico had roared at him in a voice like nobody else had:

– You!

Lowering his head Pietro gently removed the hand, with revulsion and admiration.

Since boyhood that voice had terrified him, made him ill. Then he'd cringed away, not crying but in order to be left alone. Now he felt exasperated discontent. Convinced

91

he ought not to suffer in this way he got excited by talk of justice and redemption such as he found in some propaganda leaflets lent him by the barber he went to.

He joined the Socialist Party and even founded a young socialists' club. First secretly, then bragging about it to anyone who happened to be in the restaurant. It became his ambition to write articles for a weekly called *Class Struggle*. If arrested by the police he'd have been glad. He fantasized trials, martyrdoms, conferences, the revolution. When a fellow-member called him comrade he'd have gone to the gallows for him, without a qualm.

While Domenico was increasingly taken up with his work and Poggio a' Meli. No one to help him!

In the hours of stifling heat when the restaurant remained empty the cook and the kitchen-help napped, leaning their heads against the hackstock and covering them with their aprons to keep the flies off. These hovered over the greasy dish-cloths, gathered round a dollop of gravy on the table or crawled up and down over the cuts of meat. The copper kettle simmered, a cat under the table purred. A brass tap not properly turned off leaked with a ceaseless hiss. The two tubs reflected onto the wall transparent images of the water in them, every so often traversed by the shadow of a fly.

If a customer came in the waiter took the top plate off the pile and called the cook:

– Wake up.

Then the sweat collected under his shirt went cold and the cook rubbed his ear, numb from being bent over between his arm and his head.

The restaurant resumed its stir.

Pietro spent the time off reading, hardly noticing the weather. Coming in on tiptoe Domenico caught him out:

– Why aren't you keeping an eye on the staff?

The scolding was starting again.

Once he shouted right in his ear:

– Come and get the straw weighed.

– Me?

– You.

He straightened him up, taking hold of him by the collar. But being in a hurry he went to where the men were bringing the straw in. Pietro didn't move, remaining with his head against an angle of the wall and feeling repugnance for the tears welling up.

– Another cartload coming, boss!

Said one of the two men who'd unloaded the straw already brought in.

– It's a stack!

Cried out the one pulling the cart with a rope.

– A ton!

Added Palloccola, who was holding the shafts up.

Domenico smiled at their exaggerations. He went to the new bale, fingered it and snuffed it, then without answering looked each man in the face.

In the little stable-yard the kitchen door opened on to were two other men, sweating after their work of unloading their bales and hoisting them up to the opening in the loft. Now they rested, squatting on their hunkers with their backs to the wall. Sweat dripped from their foreheads onto their dust-covered toecaps, the boot-leather crinkled and blistered.

– How much do you want?

Asked Domenico, thrusting his thumbs into his waistcoat pockets. He'd scratched the back of his hand and now and again sucked the blood off.

– How much will you give us? We want to eat too.

Answered Ceccaccio. And Palloccola:

– Those bloody farmers don't give anything away now. We're knackered.

They'd gone from farm to farm, arriving just at threshing-time, so every farmer had given them a forkful of straw to get rid of them, never refusing in case the men should steal much more in revenge.

Truth to tell they lived more by theft than by work and never had a fixed trade.

Domenico laid in large stocks of straw at discount prices, enough till the year after, for the stables attached to the restaurant.

– By weight or by eye?

Domenico asked, taking his hands from his waistcoat.

– Suit yourself. It's all the same to us.

Pipi and Nosse, who'd already done their deal with Domenico, interrupted:

– See us off first. Pay us our money.

Both were young. Pipi had a huge blown-up head with a broad brow and sky-blue eyes mild as a child's. Nosse had a black tash and lively little eyes that looked like they could bite.

– You'll help hoist this lot first.

– If you give us something to drink.

Said Pipi with a laugh and spat at the wall.

– I'm choked with dust!

Said Nosse. He stood up and then lolled against the wall again.

Domenico smiled and promised.

He had now turned fifty. His hands had grown paler, the veins mauve, with long thin fingernails that curled over.

He shaved even less often and his beard was ash-blond, nearly white. His eyes shone like oyster-shells but the extremities of the eyelids were swollen, with two magenta threads. His hair had thinned, much as he wet it with a lotion of his own inventing made from juniper berries. His moustache, extending to the cheeks, was ruffled about the mouth, giving it a good-natured look.

He had grown somewhat stooped, heavier in the shoulders, but prided himself on being as strong as ever and weighing over a hundred kilos. His arms and neck he considered practically indestructible, to be kept for use when needed.

Ceccaccio asked:

94

– By weight then?

Domenico said:

– That can't be a hundred kilos.

Ceccaccio screamed:

– Not a hundred? It's a hundred and fifty.

Palloccola added:

– We're straight we are.

He swore, but ran to untie the ropes and tip the straw off the cart. Domenico stepped forward, gripped it by the binder and lifted it, bending at the knees to gain purchase.

– I'll give you four liras. Even that's too much.

– We stole it didn't we Ceccaccio?

They all laughed, then swore and shouted, in confusion.

Nosse said:

– Pay us off then. We're going.

– Didn't you want a drink?

Asked the stableman with annoyance from the opening of the loft.

– No, no. We're dead beat. Can't help with the hoisting.

– Look at those muscles!

Said Pipi, grasping Domenico's arm: his shirt-sleeves were rolled up to the elbow.

Nosse exclaimed:

– With arms like that!

Ceccaccio said:

– Hurry up boys.

Through the half-open gate they could see the street. A young girl passed and Ceccaccio wolf-whistled.

Pipi said:

– Mind she doesn't come in here.

– What's going on? asked Domenico. Having a chat?

– What do you want done?

And Ceccaccio's mate seated himself on the straw, placing his hands on his knees.

– Weren't you two in a hurry to go just now?

– We were. Pay us off.

– Here you are: six liras. Now get out!

95

Pipi and Nosse went out with their cart.

– Our turn now.

– How much will you give?

– Let's weigh it.

The two took a steelyard, set a hook on its arm and hung the eyelet of the rope on it.

– Weigh it properly boss!

– And you don't lean your knees on it.

– Me? Look. It's half a metre off.

With the steelyard on his shoulder Palloccola raised his hands above his head, his trunk trembling with the effort.

The straw weighed a hundred kilos. They reckoned up and tied it for hoisting with the block and tackle.

– You work too boss?

– More than you do because my arms are stronger.

They all grasped the rope hanging from the pulley high up. Domenico coiled it round his wrist. As the bale rose the block creaked and they were showered with dust and straw. The stableman leaned from the opening with his arm outstretched. The men on the rope bent their backs with one heave, the bale dangled above their heads and then, seized by the stableman, swung through the opening and vanished into the dark.

– That's that!

Said Ceccaccio, wiping his neck, where bits of straw had stuck. His arms ached as though they had been racked.

Domenico had had a suspicion and he went to a heap of broken bricks and scrap iron.

– There's an old lock missing from here. Who's taken it?

The two straw-sellers glanced at each other and went on coiling their ropes.

– Now boys who's taken a lock?

Domenico asked again, pale with anger.

– I did not.

Ceccaccio answered calmly.

– I don't say you. I say it's been taken.

– What should we want with a lock?

Asked Palloccola, with hatred and resentment.

– Pipi must have taken it. He deals in scrap.

Ceccaccio said with a laugh.

– I don't know who it was. But if I did I'd get it back. It's disgraceful.

The two men grew uneasy because each was afraid the other had stolen it. But Palloccola cried out:

– Search us!

– I'm not going to search anybody. Here's your money. But I'll not buy straw from you again!

– We don't know anything about it!

Domenico saw it was impossible to find out who it was. He thought all four of them were in it. He motioned them away and went back into the restaurant.

To Pietro he said, again seizing him by the collar:

– If you paid attention as I tell you to we wouldn't get robbed.

Pietro shrugged his shoulders, thinking: *They stole because they're poor.* He walked off in the state of anxiety that came over him whenever his father was about to thrash him. Domenico did make a move at him but Rosaura held him back.

The lock had been taken the day before by a wandering beggar.

In the evening the men, stunned with fatigue, fed at a monastery and fell asleep drunk in a tavern, Pipi with his wife.

When Rosi took over *The Blue Fish* there was only one entrance, in Via dei Rossi. Flanged to the wall was an iron sign shaped like a pennant, a fish painted either side. Above the entry was a Madonna in low relief, fifteenth-century.

The lamp still hung there but the cord to let it down had gone.

Then two more entrances were made from the Via Cavour. At one, behind the plate-glass of the door-pane, was a split-level display-case lined with paper changed weekly and crammed with plucked fowls, roasted joints and other delicacies.

Past the entrance in Via dei Rossi a big gate led into an inner yard always crowded with gigs and other kinds of carriages. To one side the stables, with room for up to thirty horses. Over the stables, the hayloft.

Every Saturday Domenico had the bread left over by the customers distributed to the poor.

The top of the narrow Via dei Rossi, where the old door was, filled with beggars an hour before time. One of them was Pipi's wife, young but so skinny and sallow her mouth was a lipless slit. She walked as if unable to turn her head in any direction. Her dirty dress done up awry often showed her chest, sunken and with no breasts.

There was also an old woman with a big purple nose who had a peasant's hat of plaited straw coming undone all the way round, leaving one turn less each time. She claimed the first piece of bread and didn't go away till all of it was doled out. Sometimes she'd exclaim:

– That old bag got more than I got!

Still holding open a headscarf filled with dry bread, her stick tucked into her armpit.

To one woman Domenico gave bread three times a week. She was a big woman whose face was all one flame-colour, like a thin mask she couldn't take off, a mask of red skin. Summer and winter she wore a black woollen shawl knotted at the back. She kept her pale hands crossed over her chest. Her daughter, tall and slim, never left her side, a hand slipped under her arm. She was simple and smiled continually, but a soft wild smile.

Walking, both hugged the wall, taking long strides as

though anxious to get away. Crossing the road they hurried even more.

When they had soup at a monastery the girl would turn her back on everybody else and, taking her spoon from her mouth, mouth great soundless laughs.

When her mother died she was put in a madhouse.

There was a blind man who used to curse his son, a boy who had a wizened hand with one finger missing.

– You're a rotter! You're no help. If you stand there leaning against the wall there'll be no bread left for us. Rotter! Rotter!

He cupped his hand behind his ear, straining to make out how much was still to come, while his voice was the same as when he said his prayers.

All the others had flocked towards Rosaura like poultry towards the spot a grain of corn has bounced on.

The blind man's son listened idly, picking mortar out of the brickwork joints. He preferred being last, sure Rosaura would keep something back for him, with no need for him to argue.

The women all looked at the bread they got and one placed a piece too stale in a cavity beside the door. Leaning out Rosaura cried:

– Look at her! She comes and begs for bread and then scraps it!

One woman answered with both hands planted on her hips:

– If I'd got it I'd have eaten it!

Another laughed, biting into the bread after working it a little in her dirty hands. From the subdued and unintelligible murmur all at once a quarrel broke out:

– She comes begging for bread and she's stinking rich.

– What's it got to do with you? Me rich? . . . Take no notice of her.

Rosaura interrupted them:

– Be quiet or I won't give you any more.

Another woman, her swollen face bandaged in a blue neckcloth knotted at the back of her head, answered:

– She's right. But I've never complained.

All you could see were her two inflamed eyes, like wounds. She couldn't keep them open. To look at anything she had to lift her head sideways and as she spoke the bandage followed the movements of her mouth. And what a mouth she had!

An old man who nearly always turned up when the hand-out was over tried to arouse sympathy in the tone beggars use:

– For the love of God . . . me too.

– There's none left. Why didn't you come before?

– My legs won't carry me any more!

He struck his stick on the doorstep. Rosaura went away without giving him anything, answering:

– But they've brought you here now.

He waited a long while, with stubborn fury.

– Lady, don't make me suffer any more!

He'd worked all his life and thought it would be a godsend if he fell ill and got taken to hospital, where he could lie in bed all day. And eat well!

At least his wife had died young. She didn't suffer any more! He ended up thinking he was entitled to alms, like finding some stone steps to sit on without being moved off.

Domenico never remarried though he often considered it. He'd scrape his nails over his stubbly chin and pinch the skin of his throat, then rap on something with his knuckles, not hurting himself. After every outburst of rage he'd make a vehement and calculated announcement. Thinking

Pietro would devote himself to the business if only not to have a stepmother in the home he'd say:

– Up to you now! But you're a fool and go in for socialism. Aren't you ashamed of yourself?

He bought one hat a year and wore it daily till the brim settled on his ears, bending them down, and got greasy. He liked to wear a shirt at least a fortnight and swore when he had to have new ones made. The instinct to maintain the position he'd won drove him to pointless economies. He brought them up or rather, wishing to see them appreciated, said and it was true:

– I'm an honest man. I've sweated for my money and I mean to keep it.

He kept for luck in a wooden bowl, together with coppers, a small ancient coin the labourers had turned up while digging. Whenever it fell into his fingers he put his glasses on to see it better.

He liked it because he could scratch the metal with his nail and then it looked new. When they fetched him his glasses, after looking for them everywhere, he sat down and polished them in his filthy red handkerchief:

– I can't see it properly!

He'd go and get it examined first by the chemist, then by the antique-dealer and the barber, his nearest friends.

But of course they didn't know what it was either.

Sometimes he leant bareheaded against the restaurant door, greeting folk he scarcely knew.

In summer he had a chair brought out and dozed, till someone passing woke him with a slap on the thigh. He'd start and say:

– I'd just dropped off.

And to shake off the sleepiness go and give a few instructions.

During the day he'd eat up all the wracksy fruit and say to the cook whose black hair nearly met his eyebrows:

– Bring me an egg-dish,

He tasted it and dismissed the cook, pushing him by the arm:

– Not enough pepper in. When will you learn to do things by yourself?

The cook took offence and little by little lifted one shoulder.

– Now bring me the other one.

The cook did so and stayed to watch, standing straight with one hand on the table.

Domenico didn't wait to swallow the mouthful he took before he cried out:

– You let the garlic catch!

He wiped his moustache with his napkin and ended by saying:

– I'll have to put somebody in the kitchen with you or else get rid of you. Can't find men nowadays!

Every morning he helped himself to the leftovers from the day before, scraping the bottom of the bowls in the pantry.

But wine he drank nearly a flask of, belching into his handkerchief as he turned to the wall. Cooking smells went to his head and made him talkative. Time not spent in the kitchen he reckoned wasted, unless he was at Poggio a' Meli.

Pietro had succeeded in getting a place at the technical college in Florence, doing the preparatory work by private study in Siena, almost entirely on his own. With that every tie between father and son dissolved. Increasingly they treated each other like two strangers obliged to live together. Domenico gave up trying to exert any authority over him, thinking forbearance might make Pietro feel remorse. But he'd never forgive him now. For a whole month Domenico managed to laugh it off and both made jokes that sometimes turned into quarrels.

Pietro was still a socialist but he didn't go about with working-men so much. He was ashamed to be twenty and so behind with his studies. That was what degraded him.

In Florence he took a room in Via Cimabue, having his meals at a nearby restaurant.

He sat long hours with his head in his hands, fancying he was working, with anxiety crisscrossed and cut at all angles by bad temper and low spirits, as by lines ruled with a t-square.

He made an effort to settle down and take a liking to the college but the days seemed so disconnected, so unrelated one to another, he lost heart. The day after he couldn't recall or reassemble the events of the day before and he found it difficult to think about the days ahead.

And not getting on as well as he'd like to, not even now he was totally committed, he studied less and less!

Under his bedroom window ran the perimeter wall of a convent and in its garden, almost immediately after midday, a hundred little girls came to play games and sing songs. What sadness there was in the noise they made! Then he hated the nuns!

Whenever the girls came to the nearest corner he smiled bitterly, hoping they'd notice him. But they didn't even see he was there so then they annoyed him too.

The rumble of the city remained inaudible however as the convent wall, perpendicular to the wall of the house, ran a long way back, ending at a building so big it shut out nearly the whole of the Piazza Beccaria, while to right and left of him a crescent of other houses, though rising less high, blocked everything off.

He was ill at ease all the time, it was like not being able to make sense of something. He didn't have friends to confide in and missed having them. Everything bored him and the cupola of Santa Maria del Fiore, nearly always veiled in haze at the bottom of Via dei Servi as he returned to college after a five-minute breather in Piazza dell' Annunziata, made him droop and flag, worse if a bell rang.

The faint far-off sounds he heard about sundown made him long to be gone, as if the air were hearkening, that crystal air that made him timorous, fearful.

When he went to have dinner it was beginning to get dark. Under the trees of the Piazza Beccaria the booths of a travelling circus blinded with their acetylene flares while a roundabout went round and round to the sound of its organ.

He saw the Via Ghibellina and Via dell' Agnolo, so narrow their houses shut each other in, whereas those towards the Arezzo toll-gate break off sharp before trees and open country.

Coming in he'd find his landlady in a sewing-bee with other women he never spoke to.

Meanwhile thicker and faster, till each ran into the next, came days classes wearied him, with a weariness that had the same effect on him as an inexplicable sense of guilt.

It wasn't everyone had the means to study: he thought of that too!

In the company of his fellow-students he felt he was a young man who'd lived more than they had. It was why he called them, indulgently, boys. He smiled at their attitude to the teaching staff but couldn't bring himself to laugh at the things that amused them. Often he showed irritation, snapping their heads off.

He was all right lying on the bed with his eyes shut.

He recognized he'd failed in his attempt to take a liking to his fellow-students. Indifference towards some turned into rejection and enmity, for others he felt an aversion, especially the rich ones who looked down on him for being a socialist. Most of them thought he was scatty but nearly all liked him.

Finally, seeing nothing for it but to give in to his weariness, he stopped attending classes, telling the students, who ribbed him about it, his father couldn't afford to keep him in Florence any longer.

Towards the end he had an anxious yet also gratifying feeling he was getting more and more unlike everybody else. He couldn't make out how the others were able to study without being obliged to do as he did. It made him keener to get away.

After only four months at the college, instead of paying his landlady a month's rent in advance out of the allowance from his father, he went back to Siena, not even telling him he was coming.

He was welcomed as though he'd learned sense at last, if rather late. He didn't dare say he still wanted to prepare the exams just the same, on his own. But happening to hear from a letter Rebecca had had, that for some time Ghisola had been in Florence, wasn't at Radda any more, he took the plunge.

Domenico, whose hopes had shot up when Pietro came home of his own free will and who'd supposed a heaven-sent change of heart, tried to put a good face on it and asked:

– Why do you like it better away from your father? God must touch your heart. Don't you feel it?

But seeing even now he couldn't impose his will on him he left him to himself, sure that time was on his side.

Twinged by conscience and feeling he was right to do the opposite to what his father wanted, Pietro got down to his studies with a satisfaction he hadn't known before.

The seminary had been overlaid by the three years of technical school, a complete change. He felt quite different and about to change again.

His socialism became, as he said himself and as the fashion was, intellectual. He no longer had the faith he'd once tried to convert others with but he adopted socialist morality as his sentiments.

Those three years now seemed to have flashed by in a

single day. All their substance had gone, even the mental activity, as if they'd barely left him time to draw breath.

Despite himself, in opposition to the will he wished he had, the exams became more and more a pretext. This seemed neither legitimate nor honest. But his impatience to see Ghisola again was increasing: he was setting on her all his trust in life.

He stayed indoors for days on end, all alone, his face at the windowpane, gazing at the thin blue oblong dividing the house-tops. That remote and mindless blue almost angered him but he didn't take his eyes off it. Across it the swallows, looking black from where he stood, passed as though tossed across. Right up there, from a window at the very top, by someone he didn't even know! It was then he felt the emptiness and loneliness walled up in one of Siena's oldest mansions, wholly uninhabited, with a stumpy tower above the gloomy Arco dei Rossi, one of the dark deserted houses huddled together, bearing sculpted coats of arms, no one knew whose, of families extinct: buildings with walls two metres thick, vaulted and with almost airless rooms. Cobwebs large as dishcloths, dust on the windows permanently closed and on the sills jutting from the façades.

Sometimes, suddenly, he'd think of Florence: Ghisola, perhaps expecting him, who'd give him a bracing rebuke, the loudly rolling Arno, the always lovely hills, the mists that leave walls wet, blackening flagstones so that streets look newly paved.

His father's voice induced in him an envious melancholy and he kept away so as not to hear it, not to see him, shuddering. Why was nothing personal ever said to him? Why was he treated even now as though on sufferance? Why make useless attempts to be like the others? What were the others like?

His thoughts turned back to his fellow-students in Florence, one after the other. And why they mightn't even remember him.

How long had his mother been dead? It seemed a hundred years. Everything had turned out as it had without any need of him, behind his back.

His eyes had a mystic meekness out of keeping with the lean receding lines of his face, a discrepancy people noticed immediately.

He had those deep persistent longings, without name or purpose, that leave marks when they've passed, like you see if water has been over sand.

He'd considered himself inferior to his acquaintances in Siena but now knew this to have been a bitter mistake whose consequences, like a barren act of contrition, might extend into the future.

But why had he hoped to become a painter? What did that futile experiment signify compared with his self-respect? Could he set it aside to preserve his faith in himself?

He consoled himself by dreaming of a new way of life, unlike any before. But when? Sometimes the dream faded and he couldn't even understand how he'd come to have it.

Though fanatically sincere, no one could make him out. He felt different from what he'd been for those he was friends with before he went to Florence. He'd have liked to ask their forgiveness for not being friends with them any more but was ashamed and sorry he'd been too open with them and so easy to draw out. He reviewed the moral submissions he'd made and others had taken advantage of. In Siena he'd wanted to befriend the feeblest minds and the most unscrupulous characters, thinking them on a level with himself, as though it was a duty he had to discharge, even thinking himself wicked if he went for a walk on his own, without one of them. But since he'd been back from Florence he'd managed not to talk to anybody, wishing with a bitter fury never to see them again!

He was the youthful weakling who has bursts of energy, if misdirected.

Often in dreams he'd experienced how his feelings might

unfold, waking almost content, as though vindicated by a higher existence he couldn't put a name to.

And with what tortured joy did he anticipate the day he'd again meet the girl who already overturned his whole being!

He didn't know what he'd say to her, though he thought up expressions radiant with kindness, sometimes noticing they were meaningless words that carried his voice and soul away! Reckless unretractable words, like knives hurled hard and driven in deep, in rage. Words that unburden the self with frenetic delight and are followed by mad fears, days of storm, rains hotter and more drying than the very droughts they are supposed to drench.

Sometimes he had an urge to get himself killed, perhaps by Ghisola, who already he felt belonged to him, a delicious temptation rearisen from the past.

Spot had died of old age. They found him one February morning, under the waggon, on the threshing-floor. He'd frozen to the bricks and when Carlo knocked his belly with the shovel he was using to bury him under an olive-tree it banged like a drum. That made them laugh.

Since being castrated he'd been rather vicious. When he didn't want to be touched he first made off and then if they persisted dashed at them gnashing his teeth. He was a cross-breed half a metre high. He had the white coat that's yellow next the skin with a black spot on one ear. It's how he got his name.

When he was a pup newly weaned Domenico tied him to the well-head and whenever he howled the farm-hands were ordered to kick him.

Later he bought him a brass-studded collar, never taken

off except while he was being clipped.

He could hear Domenico's horse's bells when it was still in the suburb outside the Porta Camollia. Then he went out into the roadway and started barking. When the horse came into sight at a turning not far from the gate he ran to and fro between one point and another. People stepped aside but quite a few kids not quick enough got knocked down by him.

But after eating he raced through the fields leaving marks wherever he went, specially in standing corn, where a lane was left you could see a long way off. At seed-time they had to pelt him with stones because where he went jumping about the work had to be done all over again. He liked ripe grapes and, better still, figs.

The only ones he obeyed were Domenico and Giacco. Others he was merely afraid of, unless provoked to bite, like he did Ghisola once when she sat astride him.

No other dog was a match for him and several he'd killed by fanging the spinal cord. Two he tore to pieces because they went to eat the dinner in his dish.

He tolerated cats however, so long as they didn't come too near. But he wouldn't have them round at all when basking in the sun. Then he kept one eye shut and the other open, opened the first and shut the other, all at once springing up with a deafening bark.

Even as a puppy he wasn't playful. His behaviour varied with whoever it was approaching him and he was never wrong. He wouldn't obey Pietro and never fawned on him.

When they buried him, after telling Domenico, who remembered he'd only cost two liras and gave instructions to keep the collar, Giacco wept. He felt old too and looking at the carcass said to the other men:

– That is how we'll end.

Enrico answered:

– He was past it. What use are old crocks?

He looked at Carlo, who laughed.

109

But Giacco threw his mattock aside, crying out:

– I'll live longer than you will, mind! See this poor brute? He had a kinder heart than you've got!

– I didn't mean you.

– Who then? My head's not what it was but I've still got sense.

Carlo began to swear and take it out on the dog.

– Not past it? Then we wouldn't have had to dig the hole or had this quarrel. No point in losing our tempers over a dead dog!

He made out he was angry but was glad it was Giacco who'd gone white in the face like that, leaving him out of it. Giacco kept his eye on the dog to make sure the others didn't tread on him out of spite or inattention.

Masa came to see him buried, halting a little distance from the hole and chewing without stop, though she felt queasy. When they'd finished she punched her stomach and said:

– If I eat any more I'll get my guts clewed up.

Giacco raised his head and glared at her:

– You think it's funny then? Get back to your chores. You'd sooner croak than stop eating. Don't you know it drives me mad?

Masa pocketed her crust and answered:

– What a crosspatch you are, God knows!

She sighed and continuing to walk in front of the others added to herself:

– Patience, patience!

She didn't know what they'd been saying to her husband.

It was Domenico who'd sent Ghisola away from Poggio a'

Meli. A shrewd precaution, he'd seen her flighty carry-on and wanted to stay out of trouble.

She'd gone to Poggio a' Meli when she was twelve and when she came back to Radda she was seventeen.

Other members of the family were hardly more than names to her and she'd not seen her two sisters since she'd left. Not having lived together they felt no affection for her but went to meet the coach, wearing new shoes and their Sunday head-shawls.

She'd brought each of them a pinchbeck ring as a present. They kissed her and then both felt bashful. They weren't sure she belonged and kept changing places as they walked. In fact the younger one dropped behind and when Ghisola called her to come beside her went along the bank instead, on the grass verge, dropping her head whenever Ghisola turned round because she didn't want her to see she was looking. The elder sister didn't say much either, nothing really.

When they reached home, where the parents were waiting, Ghisola began to cry. But they had a good dinner, there was fried rabbit and chicken: two hens that shouldn't have been culled, because still in lay, their ovaries fat and full. The bread was fresh that morning.

Borio di Sandro, a widower friend of the family who helped out with expenses, had brought a flask of his best wine. The slight fuddle smoothed over their differences, that first day.

But Ghisola jibbed at doing the sort of work her sisters did and between themselves they called her *the delicate young lady*. She avoided being with them and whenever she could went afield by herself. They didn't dislike her but she always contrived to cut short any conversation they tried to start. To mass too she went by herself and her thoughts drifted back to Poggio a' Meli. Coming back to Radda had been disagreeable enough: only Borio understood that. She was always telling him she wasn't going to stay and get bored to death.

A year later, the evening after a religious festival, he'd accompanied her to a procession through the village.

It was a procession of local farmers walking hat in hand behind a small cross, two by two. After the men came the girls, bunched together, singing out of books held open with both hands and keeping their heads down, like when you walk into a blustery wind. Then another cross, big and black and covered in dust, with a crown of thorns on top and rope scourges dangling. Then the priest.

The widower saw Ghisola home, as she'd never encouraged any of the young fellows, considering herself a cut above them.

They left the village by a road going sharp downhill and getting darker and darker, alongside lines of dense cypresses, then across country. They struck a steep track going halfway up a big tump overhung with tall oaks.

Ghisola, who liked Borio, was walking one step ahead, rather sad as often happens after the exceptional and sort of compulsory merriment of a holiday.

– Why won't she look at me now?

He threw away his cigar, it was making his mouth nasty and his head muzzier. They were alone! Everybody else had gone off somewhere! True, he sometimes heard steps, before she did, but then the trampling went away.

Ghisola seemed to be trying to shrink into herself. She walked along almost unseeing and but for Borio, who kept close behind her, she could hear him breathing, would have bumped into an embankment.

From time to time she stumbled. Her legs felt numb and seemed so long, every step she took stunned her. Then she thought she'd better stop. She reckoned she'd had too much to drink. Her head was swimming and without noticing she was doing it she sighed, long and deep, heaving her stomach.

Dusk, with the moon palpitating behind a veil of cloud, filled every corner with flimsy see-through shadows. He took her hand: she let him take it. He felt Ghisola had

112

become an almost ludicrously feeble creature. But he understood. He kissed her. Startled, she drew away. He kissed her again, afterwards looking hard at the nape of her neck and the hollow between the shoulder-blades. Perhaps he wouldn't get a chance to kiss her again! But as she didn't turn round he clasped her about the waist.

She kept quiet! She was afraid to speak, afraid too of the cypress shadows that, just outside the village, unexpectedly crossed the road and climbed up again, like they were alive, with their tips over the top of the wall opposite.

Suddenly she slumped on a slab-stone halfway along the track, hiding her face in the shawl slipped from her hair and holding over it hands that looked made of iron, like the tines of a pitchfork.

Wanting to say something to her, though not knowing what, he had to bend right down. He didn't feel he was beside the Ghisola he'd known so long and who'd been with him just before. She pressed her legs one against the other, tight, so together they looked like an upturned plough.

After a silent tussle, his hands against hers, already feeling the remorse, without any passion, Borio brought out:
– Yes I tell you . . . Yes I tell you . . .

Their fingers were sweaty and slippy. He had an urge to twist hers off. They stared at each other like people do when about to quarrel because now they can't stop.

She opened her legs. Then she wept.

Being older, Borio was able to command a certain deference from her. He had a big dome with a bump on the top. He was clean-shaven and close-cropped but his hair came down to his temples and his eyebrows were like long black

113

bristles set together above the nose.

Next day it was she came to see him, she became possessive.

Her eyes always looked tender now and her hair softer, over the low forehead.

Borio was gone on her and would have married her. But the farm-manager he worked for had her too and being jealous each of them ran her down, whoever he was talking to. So lots of the young fellows she'd rejected wouldn't leave her alone.

They went after her in the fields, under the fig-trees and the peach-trees, they lay in wait for her when she came back through the juniper-bushes. She had to defend herself tooth and nail, crying and running indoors for refuge. Then she got the giggles and watched for them to pass by under her window. One or two even tried to shin over the wall. Then they threw stones at the gate.

The farm-manager wanted to take pot-shots at them, like at hares.

But to avoid scoldings from her parents day in day out, and to be more independent, she found herself a place as a maid to a lady at La Castellina, another village a few kilometres from Radda.

The road, downhill till you come to a mill-race, climbs between winding and spiralling lines of hills all similar to one another and of the same gentle gradient, with rows of vines between drystone walls, farmhouses behind cypresses and an occasional bell-tower so far away, a bend in the road and it's gone. And the more the road turns upon itself, as if tormented by its own length, losing patience, the quieter it becomes and the drier and lonelier the countryside.

There are flat hill-tops, stone-flagged, covered with brushwood, and a few crosses made of vine-stakes, some of them fallen down, alongside track for men and beasts.

Oak coppices but thinned out and in between the foliage glimpses of the salients and re-entrants of other hills, steep descents levelling out abruptly where three or four slopes join rolling grassland, terraces of rust-red earth or rock-faces.

Past Fonterutoli, a hamlet like an angle of houses with four shops, the road gets very very steep and reaches its high point.

Sometimes the whole of a wood shows breadthways and a bird flies across it. From an old chipped runnel, the only one there is on this road, water splashes into a massy trough.

The silence of those woods, for hours and hours on end! It's like the silence of the rocks locked in the grip of the tree-roots. But when the wind blows from the direction of the other hills and these film over, the contortions of the boughs are frightening, they roar and whistle. The branches gather themselves in, drawing their leaves together, and when they re-open a tremble goes all through the wood, occasionally accompanied by a sound that leaps from place to place, plaintive and melodious. Twigs snap, leaves smack on stone-pits, birds fly hither and thither as though wind-blown.

When the storm breaks the oaks stoop, all together, straining themselves, to duck. Overhead the clouds stop, as if staying to watch, and even the wind doesn't seem able to move them.

Sometimes the oaks keep still and then the clouds go by.

Leaving the village the road makes a dog-leg uphill, a sliver of white between two plats of green, then plunges straight down for over a kilometre, hewn between blocks of rock, and from there the whole of La Castellina comes into view at the bottom.

At this point other hills not much higher continue to the right while to the left they sink lower and lower to become the floor of the Val d'Elsa, with villages like little clusters of tumbledown masonry. Then the Montagnola and Montemaggio take their rise and behind them other ranges stretch out, high up indistinguishable from distant

115

clouds.

Here you nearly always come upon a flock of sheep toddling across the bare patch to browse the other side. Or they descend a path, one behind the other, as if pitched head foremost and dragged down by the weight of the one leading.

All those red-painted ox-carts and, squatting atop the oxen, the farmers, most of them, taking it easy!

An infrequent motorcar, one of the first in fact, would bring to doors and windows all who were quick enough, amazed it should drive through just as though they weren't there. Then they'd exchange the usual glance and go back to what they'd been doing. What speed!

The women who had babies crawling about, almost in the middle of the roadway, hurled curses.

One of those retired managers who've done well out of farming would flatten himself against the wall harder than he needed to and vent his spleen to his cronies as he sat on a stool, his peeled ashplant between his legs and his back at an angle to the cords and ropes and whips hung up outside the shop, which also sold sulphur, brushes and hobnails.

There he'd sit two solid hours, always spitting to the same side and getting a passing boy to buy him his cigar, so as not to have to move.

– They ought to be put in prison didn't they? There was none of that nonsense in our time.

He laughed, opening his mouth so wide you could see the whole length of the groove in his tongue, a tongue pared to a point.

At midday, when the sun's heat increased the silence, he'd wait watch in hand for the bells to ring:

– What time do you make it?

The bells moved and everyone stood up as though taken by surprise, as though the walls too were going to change position. Shops shut at once. Men who lived outside the village went to have lunch but loitering in the sunshine, like dogs that wag their tails at all comers.

116

The top half of the tower was inside the sun's orb and must it seemed be blazing like a flame.

When the bells stopped there was one that could still be heard at a distance, lost in the undergrowth, continuing on its own and mingling its ringing with the tinkling of the sheep-bells.

A girl from the next village brings with her all its prejudices, its likes and dislikes. And in Ghisola's case there was a lot of tittle-tattle and amusement.

The priest, obviously tipped off by the one at Radda, reprimanded the lady who'd taken her on. In him Ghisola sensed a fanatical persecutor. She could tell by the drawn drained look on his face whenever he looked at her, twisting his mouth askew, with myopic gimlet eyes. At that she walked with more of a lascivious strut, like a duck holding its beak up.

How she hated Radda now! No, Borio wouldn't do it to any other girl, to one of her sisters for instance!

She saw the whole procession over again or rather she amused herself by identifying, one by one, saying their names in her head, the men who'd been singing without taking notice of her, following that naked worm-eaten crucifix, with blobs of red paint like real blood. How she wished it would crash to the ground and crack the crowd's clogs! The procession seemed to be swaying, coming straight into her eyes! The canopy slightly awry and the music re-echoing as though the winding valley resonated shell-wise, the singing almost speech and the bells clanging so loud each one sounded distinct.

Ghisola had thought she'd find people in La Castellina who wouldn't bother so much about her but it was no different.

Everybody knew something and anybody who didn't made something up.

The mayor grew uneasy, it was becoming quite scandalous. He took to saying certain women are all very well in towns but not in villages. And in La Castellina

117

of all places! But he liked Ghisola, indeed paid her attentions.

Though she had several admirers she couldn't make friends with any because as soon as the two of them spoke to each other there was always someone who found out and went round telling. So then there was no way they could get together again.

As for the young gentlemen, for them it was excellent entertainment and each one put it about she was his mistress.

The half-dozen young ladies, deep down, envied her for being so popular with the men, who gave her a bad name but did look at her.

It got too much for Ghisola and she had to get away from La Castellina too: *what was she doing up there in that gossip-shop?*

Within less than a month, by means of contacts with female friends and a go-between, she was taken by an ironmonger separated from his wife and just wanting to meet that kind of girl. Finding her to his liking and agreeable to the suggestion he set her up in a small house he had outside Badia a Ripoli, near Florence, where everyone called him plain *signor Alberto*.

Sending her address home Ghisola told them she'd found a place in service.

That suited Ghisola better and that's how she was living when Pietro, in Florence for the exams, paid her a visit.

He rang at the little door, its pale-blue paintwork sun-crackled. The china number-plate gleamed pure white in the sunshine and the numbers, dark blue, jigged and writhed.

118

He heard a scurry of footsteps, then a woman's voice the instant the door opened. He stepped up quickly, breathing hard, as though he'd inhaled more air than could get through his nostrils and it had liquefied.

– Is Ghisola in?

Her curiosity aroused and smiling at his embarrassment the woman gave the answer any one would:

– I'll call her.

The first impression he had didn't tally with his expectation: there was a sort of hostility. He didn't let it worry him but tried to recall the photograph and what it had made him feel.

The woman went away, dragging her slipshod feet, and Pietro was left alone in the sudden silence. He wished he wasn't there, his sense of himself seemed to have no connection either with the place or with Ghisola. Was it really she who was living there?

Through a chink of the venetian blind a ray of sunlight pierced to the centre of the room, diffusing bright calm. But the silence baffled him, it seemed like an abyss, an ambush. Even so he felt cheerful. He heard a few quick steps: it was Ghisola.

Recognizing him she smiled and blushed, then only the smile remained. Looking at her didn't seem to enable him to see her face and he couldn't bring himself to utter a conventional greeting.

So she touched him on the hand and asked him to sit down, leaning against the table and waiting for him to say something.

For a moment she was disconcerted, feeling an impulse to cry, but she controlled herself so that he could see straight off she was prettier now.

The streak of sunlight resting on her skirt enhanced the brightness.

His good Ghisola! He'd found her again! He sprang to his feet, managing to ask, with his eyes on the wall:

– How long have you been here?

She told him in a casual manner Pietro found objection-
able and clasping her hands in front of her asked:

– Are you engaged?

– No.

But he was prompted (who knows why?) to tell her a
fib.

– But I know you are.

She made a sly face and as though she'd mentioned
something that put her in good humour added:

– Do you think I haven't inquired about you?

Pietro couldn't speak for contentment.

She noticed and about her eyes and mouth a mark
of tenderness showed. So Pietro, thinking this the right
moment, said, without looking at her:

– I've been thinking about you all the time.

Ghisola turned towards the door. Her skirt moving, the
streak of light looked itching to be off. Pietro whispered:

– Do you think that woman can hear us?

That's just what Ghisola had suspected but she cheered
up thinking what laughs they'd have afterwards: helpless
with laughter they'd clutch each other's arms. She nearly
forgot to answer but seeing his embarrassment said:

– She might be listening. It doesn't matter.

– Who is she? Why's she with you here?

She wasn't short of a lie and after putting her tongue
out, as much as to say: *What a lot you want to know!*,
answered:

– She's the friend of the lady I work for.

– Does your mistress live alone?

– All by herself except for this companion. She never lets
a man in.

– And you like it here? How does she treat you? Do you
have to work very hard?

– Oh she loves me!

He thought: *She's grown fond of her, it was the same before,
with Giacco and Masa.* Shyly and out of consideration for
her he said:

– Would your mistress suspect you of something if she found me here? Where is she now?

– She'll be coming back later than usual today. I'll have to tell her you've been.

– Tell her. She won't be cross with you. You mustn't tell lies.

He meant about their relation to each other. At the same time it made him wonder, the way the place was run and the behaviour of the woman Ghisola was so unconcerned about. But he reminded himself too she had to work for her living. Then a scruple held him back: he couldn't offer her his love at once in case she took offence. She'd worked on his father's farm and might not trust him. But overcome by impatience he asked:

– And you, have you thought about me at all?

With these words he felt re-attached to his sense of himself, believing Ghisola was included in it too. It was necessary to tear her away from these people he didn't know, who were keeping her to themselves!

He fell silent and she made one of those grimaces that reveal a fleeting glimpse of an entire life-style. Pietro didn't catch on but asked:

– And no one has ever loved you?

She didn't answer. He repeated the question. Still she didn't, and he thought he'd gone too far, for the first time. But she ought to be immediately sincere! He wondered if he could talk to her as trustingly as he used to and felt strongly drawn to the sudden silence, having no previous experience of such snares.

She waited for him to lift his head, with a look on her face half-indulgent half-astute, then asked with an almost jocular air:

– Do you like me now?

He refrained from answering, feeling a profound happiness.

Outside them and the room nothing else existed!

Ghisola went on:

– Are you still in love with me?

Then he answered, speaking with an effort, as though he'd got somebody else's voice:

– If you've never been loved!

There was a silence such that each thought they could hear the creaking of their joints and they avoided each other's eyes.

He was sorry for her, for being a servant who might be humiliated with a scolding when her mistress came to hear of his visit. He went to the window, shifted the green blind and saw in blazing sunshine flower-beds with a bamboo centre-piece. Ghisola leapt to his side and drew him back:

– Don't look out of the window!

He took fright as though the bricks round the window were all coming apart and it was his fault. But when Ghisola touched him he felt himself turn pale. As once before!

Stepping aside at once, before he could recover, she said with a laugh:

– You do still love me. It's true.

Pietro laughed to copy her, feeling his head reel, as when a danger is past. Ghisola put on an air of disbelief and added:

– But I haven't been the only one!

He was incapable of any kind of premeditation and the words he spoke were carried on an unconscious stream:

– Why do you say that? If I tell you . . .

Even his hands, it seemed to him, spoke. All at once he had a perception of Ghisola far far away, beyond all illusion, with an inimical premonition he'd have to fight to call her to him. His dream of loving was still distant! How deep he'd dreamed!

He couldn't tell her she was beautiful in case it should sound a questionable compliment and also because being beautiful would be worthless unless she had a deep-rooted instinct of honesty as well, like he had.

He wanted her to realize she was honest and be proud of

it. This was necessary, on principles of morality he merged into principles of redemption and justice in day-to-day life. So he had first to set an example. He decided to explain it to her later on.

He couldn't think of anything else to say and somebody seemed to be directing him to go. He took up a position in the middle of the room, glanced at Ghisola, extended his hand to her and slowly went out: not knowing how to, barging into the door-jamb. She was glad the visit had ended so soon, signor Alberto might be coming in.

The stairs were faced with tiles worn thin and concave and as he looked down at them his feet seemed to be treading them in.

He was shaken by a heavy shudder. He shut the door with a thud he thought too loud, raised his eyes and saw Ghisola looking out from a cast-iron balcony. She signalled goodbye with a movement of her head. He hadn't the strength to signal back. Twice he turned round, wishing he was there with her, overflowing with tenderness and thinking it less than ever possible to leave with a conventional phrase. He came into Florence unaware how he'd got back.

Though walking on the footway by the embankment wall he didn't look at the Arno, its low water a muddy green with a few streaks of peacock blue. Grounded on a spit of its bed lay some barges laden with sand and round these the river, shallower than anywhere else, twitched and twinkled.

Sometimes the hum of the city sounded further away, removed elsewhere to return a moment later, and as he was walking fast he had now and again to stop, having missed his way.

He reached the Lungarno degli Archibusieri, the Ponte Vecchio with its twin piers supporting the goldsmiths' workshops batched together, as well as the shops perched on arched trusses and red-painted timber struts, their walls reduced to shreds by windows too wide and too close together.

On the further bank old grey grimy houses squeezing close up, as though afraid of being pulled down, houses like thin strips of various colours clinging to those on the bridge: oblongs of building and oblongs of water, all continuous but dissimilar.

The Arno lapped the undersides of the trusses. Its silence and the silence of the houses allowed distant murmurings to be heard, nearly always in tune with a bell. The cypresses of Torre al Gallo high in the sky, with the softest possible motionlessness.

On the hither bank half-closed shops scorched by the sun, in the torrid shade of their short blinds, and streets running empty into the city.

While from the church of San Miniato and the Belvedere trees stretch like a high hedgerow broken by white villas sinking behind the roofs of Borgo San Iacopo.

The Poggio dell' Incontro had a bright blue.

On the Ponte Vecchio wind flapped the goldsmiths' faded awnings and lifted the dust of the streets onto the river. And now the gleaming statues, with their ochre shadows, of Ponte Santa Trinità, its bridgehead between the apse of the riverside church of San Iacopo and the church of Cestello. Then the bell-tower of Santo Spirito, in front of buildings rising less high and more spaced out, as far as the chimneys of the Pignone. And, almost by itself, the Ponte della Carraia and in the background the first trees of the Cascine, in the sun and far away.

It was very late when he got back to his digs. He rearranged the books he'd brought from Siena and unpacked his clothes. Twice or thrice in the night he woke up and before falling asleep again said to himself, each time ecstatically, out loud:

– Not long till tomorrow!

He dithered all morning and later in the day wrote to her, he felt he really loved her. He couldn't recall her face, it was rather that its movements seemed to repeat themselves round him without being clearly seen. The colour of her dress had turned into light that from time to time broke into a flash.

Ghisola got her lover to read her the letter. She'd already told him about the visit, after her fashion, not trusting Beatrice's tongue. Beatrice was the housemaid Pietro had seen.

Signor Alberto asked with a laugh:

– What does he write to you for? He seems to have been in love with you a long time. It's a funny letter. Let me read it again.

This time he stopped after each sentence to glance up at Ghisola, who was leaning on his shoulder. They condemned the sentiments the letter expressed, knowing these were beyond them. When he finished he gave her a kiss:

– That's one for him.

She tore the letter up and to entertain him further, but also out of an elation all her own, began walking about on her heels and executing turns. He was amused but asked:

– How come you're so keen on him?

– Because.

She made another sentimental body-roll.

– You're not telling me everything.

He took hold of her ear and asked under his breath:

– With him too?

She straightened up and went pale, answering as promptly as she could:

– I swear I haven't. But if he marries me why should you mind?

Then he could back out!

– I only want to be sure for your sake he's really in love with you. And well-off, the sort you've dreamt of. Otherwise I think you might as well stay where you are.

– Well-off? His father's got ten farms and a big restaurant.

– But has he given his consent?

125

– I expect he sent him.

Signor Alberto believed her and was satisfied.

While she was taking the plates from the sideboard to set them on the table he thought he might, if the fancy took him, stay on as her lover.

But business wasn't good and he had to put aside that life of idle ease.

Ghisola was keeping him under watch when absent-mindedly he lowered his head. She waited for his inmost thought, the one he might conceal, but fearing he might go on thinking too long said:

– What's the matter with you this evening? Is it your nerves again?

He smiled and replied:

– You're right. I'm too old for you, you'd be throwing yourself away. Get yourself a husband. I want you to.

– Why do you have to bring that up? Is there any need to? You make me wild.

– It's you who brought it up, Ghisola dear. But I've got a brainwave.

– Tell.

– You go about it so as to make him think afterwards he's the one who's made you pregnant. It won't be difficult. Like it?

She bit her lip quickly with her back to the light and ran a finger round the rim of her plate.

– Well? he asked.

– I won't even answer him. If he comes back here I'll throw a bucket of water over him.

And she pressed the electric buzzer to tell Beatrice to bring supper in. Signor Alberto, as if winding up his reflections, exclaimed:

– You'll be better off than I will.

Adding with a certain gravity:

– Only don't let him come to my place . . .

Feeling on slippery ground she turned her head.

– . . . to do your stuff.

126

She laughed. Then he became sad:

– And I don't want the Badia people to see you here with him. They know me.

Mentally he went on: *I lose her too: had to, apparently*. He tried to smile, stroked his moustache, went to look her in the eye and gave her a pinch that hurt.

– Understand?

She laughed so as not to cry. He had no desire to get soft and asked with mock-shyness:

– Can't you get him to . . . kiss you?

Adding as a joke:

– He's craftier than I am. Because you've done whatever you liked with me.

They burst out laughing and, the maid coming in, sat down to supper.

Flattered to realize all of a sudden how much Pietro loved her Ghisola didn't send a reply to his letter but went to see him herself. Mightn't he marry her after all? Then she'd return to Siena not as a girl from the country but as lady of the house.

When she arrived Pietro was sitting in his room holding a book, not studying but rolling the edges of the pages round his fingers. He'd only taken one of the two exams and was thinking about Ghisola. He wasn't meant to sit the exams! This was what he was meant to do!

When she opened the door without so much as knocking his heart jumped. He exclaimed:

– Come in! I was expecting you.

Demurely she seated herself and turned her veil up to her hat trimmed with artificial violets. He said:

– Take it off.

127

He'd never spoken to a woman like that before!

As though she knew, or could tell from his voice, she smiled amiably and, after examining everything with assumed diffidence, stepped to the looking-glass, drew out the hatpin, rested it in her mouth and laid it together with the hat on the marble of the wash-stand.

Being married already! How lovely she was!

They sat face to face, he feeling an awkward pleasure in smiling at her and she taking care to do what he did. They brought their hands together across the little table and he squeezed her fingers, one after another, in silence, as if to persuade her there was no harm in it.

The sun reddened the slats of the closed window-shutters.

He stood up and kissed her and she half-shut her eyes. At the same time he'd have liked to reprove her: *You can trust me, but suppose I didn't really love you?* He held her hands tight to show her he loved her, liking the smell of her sweat.

Ghisola lowered her eyelids whenever her eyes met his but smiled at him, inviting him to understand and stop loving her that way, making out she'd never been any-one's. Then she coughed and leant back in the chair to put distance between them.

So she was his! But what did he give her in return for all that joy? He asked:

– Can you love me too?

Ghisola bent her head without answering. He insisted on being answered, with a gentleness he wished her to appreciate. It was then she kissed him for the first time, doing it as though she didn't know how to and afterwards dabbing her mouth with her hanky as though sorry she'd done it. Quickly and lightly she said:

– I've got to be back.

Pietro thought: *Indeed it's just as well she's not staying long.*

He asked permission to kiss her again and Ghisola pretended to scold him for not asking permission before, humiliating him, he didn't know what to say in reply. The black of her pupils had the swimmy look things have deep under water.

Putting her hat on she pricked her finger with the hatpin.

She could get hurt even though he was there! He grasped her hand, watched the blood-drop grow larger and, when it was about to fall, sucked it.

She submitted, intrigued, and smiled at him as at a small boy, with a gentleness that was more intimate and more indulgent.

Enraptured Pietro said:

– I'll remember this always!

In Piazzo Beccaria, and from the way the trees swayed in the breeze it seemed they oughtn't to go any further, the handkerchief dropped from her hand. He picked it up and kept it till they separated. It was practically the same thing as her clothes.

– When will you come again?

Ghisola wasn't sure signor Alberto really would have her do what he wanted, not immediately.

– I don't know . . .

Pietro tried to work out if he ought to think that good or bad. At least it seemed she couldn't be going away.

– Tomorrow?

But he didn't like to insist, not being sure it wasn't a blunder.

– That's too soon. In five days' time.

She smiled to temporise.

– Remember I'll be waiting. Don't you believe me? Tell me you do.

– I know.

She smiled again.

– May I write to you? But can you read?

– No.

She'd have liked to lie and look at him proudly but she blushed, dropping her head.

– Who'll read the letters to you? A woman, yes? . . .
Mind you only let a woman read you them.

– A woman, of course. Do you have to tell me?

And she curled down her nether lip. Pietro gazed at her
enchanted and then, to make sure she wasn't being forced
into telling him a lie, asked:

– The one I saw when I called?

But Ghisola twigged and laughed, answering:

– A different one. Don't come any further.

He said:

– Come again soon.

Instantly it occurred to him: *Why do I do as she tells me?
But it gives me pleasure and makes me feel proud.*

She went, not turning round once. He stood and
watched her disappear from sight round a bend in the
road where a cypress rose erect above the wall. She was like
a stranger who knew nothing of their love, whereas what
he'd experienced seemed more real to him than Ghisola
herself.

A leaf falling from a garden-tree brushed his face. If he'd
been at Poggio a' Meli he'd have kept it.

As soon as her back was turned Ghisola thought she'd
been wasting time, that's all.

Day after day Pietro expected to see her sitting there
once more with her arms on the little table. A conviction grew in him that he'd found her again but wasn't
in love with her. He cut his exams though he thought
about them continually and had a terrifying hallucination
where he saw himself being questioned and not being able
to answer.

Instead, tearful with impatience, he went to see her.

130

Ghisola opened the door herself and Pietro was surprised to find he did love her as soon as he asked:

– Were you expecting me?

She hedged.

– Maybe.

Though feeling a kind of aversion to speaking he found himself saying:

– Can't we go for a walk together? Are you free?

Ghisola considered and then answered:

– Wait for me in front of the abbey.

Her consenting gave Pietro no pleasure. He was oppressed by an uneasy sense of a lie he couldn't put his finger on. He only waited for her so as to keep to the suggestion he'd made.

It was windy but everything burnt under the July sun. Some cypresses along the Bisarno road swayed. The light seemed continually being altered by the wind. A line of olive-trees stretched their branches along a wall and their tops, of a tender green, kept beating against it. Their shadows too looked like tree-tops, hard to tell from the real ones.

She came walking briskly, bareheaded and wearing round her neck a chain with a small gold heart-shaped locket.

Pietro was afraid he'd make himself ridiculous if he told her he'd got to go back to Siena. But in the end she asked him, after walking along in silence while he kept his eyes on her hands:

– When are you leaving?

– Tomorrow.

– So we shan't see each other again!

Surprised at her rather playful calmness he asked with a sigh:

– Will you think of me all the time?

Ghisola answered with conviction, almost with compliance:

– All the time.

She looked at him and seeing his dissatisfaction went on:

– You think I don't love you very much.

Though that was true he answered:

– I trust you.

Holding her head down Ghisola smiled again but this time her mouth was slow in performing the action.

The road, where at points the wind raised swirls of white dust without itself being felt, was as lonely as though no one had ever been along it. He thought Ghisola goodlooking in a different way, more buxom: *Yes, even like this she's well-dressed.* But he couldn't remove his eyes from the locket. He wanted to take it from her, otherwise she'd get looked at straight between the breasts.

Ghisola noticed and waited. When he saw she'd noticed he said:

– Why are you wearing it?

She blushed and seemed to want to protect it.

– Did you buy it yourself or was it a present?

– A present.

– Tell me who gave it to you. At once.

He stopped in front of her, obliging her to stop too.

– My sister Lucia.

– How long ago?

– Last year, when she came to see me.

– She's fond of you?

– Yes, but I don't like her.

– Why not?

– I don't know . . .

– Why not? Tell me. If you don't tell me!

– I don't know. We have different characters.

He thought this might be true, because physically they were quite unlike, and was glad. All the same he was jealous even of her sister. He said:

– I'll buy you one and you can wear mine. Or rather yours, because nothing's mine now. Agreed?

Actually she felt like laughing but it was obviously not the moment. Instead she turned on her heel without saying anything. And as she started walking fast as though late for something he asked:

– Is that lady expecting you?

– Yes, we've been taking a chance.

– But why say that if I really love you? You mustn't let it worry you.

She smiled and quickened her step without answering.

Pietro let her enter the square by herself and then, pretending to be waiting for someone, strolled round. There was nobody there! He saw a dog lolloping off with its bony back arched.

On the Grassina road he looked at the hill, a pale faded green, all of it olive-groves with slim cypresses mixed in here and there.

A tram coming round the turning he got in. When he looked up he was already in Florence, just past the toll-gate, on the gleaming Lungarno, and from there saw all the bell-towers in a single glance.

Pietro was so worked up he thought: *Even if she's had to give herself so as not to go hungry I couldn't take advantage of it. I'd cry. I'd help her to change. Then somebody might respect her and marry her. But she would have told me. Why shouldn't she have?*

Despite the doubt he thought her wonderfully pure. That made him want to possess her and he cried. *She's got to be mine! I want to be the one to love her! Why shouldn't I?* Wasn't it his moral duty too? But how find somewhere better to live than in his father's house? Ghisola had said:

– He's rich. It all depends on him. But he's sure to say no.

Domenico didn't even answer when Pietro came back from Florence, told him he loved Ghisola and if it was

133

agreeable to him had decided to marry her. But he was stung to fury, like a vixen when they've set fire to straw in her earth.

Neither mentioned the exams, Pietro to keep the truth from him, Domenico to prevent Pietro bothering about them any more but with an urge to fling him against the wall like a cushion.

Pietro came home from long solitary walks in the country, having sought counsel of the sky. At times he thought Ghisola couldn't possibly have made love with anyone, it would have tainted her looks. It was he who was suspicious!

Other times he wondered: *Am I really in Siena? It looks altered. Surely the sky's bluer, it usedn't to be like this.* He noticed that on summer evenings a pale warm light lingers in the Piazza del Campo, a residue of noon, like the light of a lantern that only illuminates its own interior, and that the people crossing the open space look remote in time, in an eerie silence.

– When Ghisola's here I'll tell her what I feel.

Every morning he woke up sighing. And how well he remembered his dreams!

But he couldn't live without Ghisola and about the middle of August made up his mind to go and fetch her. She could go home to Radda and stay there till the wedding: perhaps a year, eighteen months at the most. Why wouldn't he get consent? Meanwhile having her stay at Radda he'd feel more sure of her.

He borrowed the fare from Rebecca.

During the few hours he spent in Florence he seemed to be still in Siena, at the top of the Via di Camporegio, where he'd passed every day when he went to the technical school. It's only a step from the rough ruddy pile of San Domenico to the houses that clamber higgledy-piggledy round the Cathedral, stopping underneath as soon as they meet it, but looking down from there into the deep void of Fontebranda, it catches your breath.

He'd see the Ospedale, high on the city walls, go from blood-red to the colour of burnt earth and the sky from indigo to grey. Then the first stars, here and there: poignant, they were so sparse.

The alleys, looking like enormous cracks and fissures, went black.

Down among the walled gardens and orchards, each one higher than the next, often with party-walls, and down into the salients and re-entrants of the hills, adjusting itself to their unequal gradients, twilight seemed to fall like when it pours with rain.

A drunk would start singing and then break off. The Costaccia like the parapet of a precipice and the Costone with an almost sheer drop, its solid broad-backed arch holding it steady so that another road can run over it, tilt up towards the houses.

No two roofs the same height, not even if next to each other. Houses in clusters large and small, drawn out in parallel lines, slanting and twisting. Sometimes they stand at two or three interlocking angles, in rings, in knots, closed up, mixed up, entangled, in curves broken or flattened, always with abrupt changes due to the shapes of the hills, the slopes and bends of the roads, the squares that from high up look like holes.

All at once a gap between two houses, then other houses that grip each other and hold on tight, pressing and sinking, then rising and turning to vanish from view behind houses that have a quite different rhythm and come from the opposite side. Paths climbing uphill but these too stop short or turn into a broad irregular fan of spokes, quite flat or out of shape, where houses perch precariously,

135

sideways, crossways, any way they happen to or are able to, being pushed by others that give the effect of trying to find a place to settle in, each for itself.

Squat houses almost sinking into the ground, in Porta Ovile, Fontebranda and Tufi, shore up houses that overlook them, restrain them from spreading themselves thinner. The highest points seem trying to attract the houses that fear of loneliness has forced to give in.

Where the terrain rises a whirling hurly-burly appears, where it dips the houses tumble on top of one another like a rock-slide. Or you can count up to ten long rows of roofs, higher and higher, beside rows going at right angles to them.

Out of all this jumble the Mangia Tower rises placid.

And all round the city olives and cypresses squeeze in between the houses, as though having come in from the country they didn't want to go back.

In Florence he seemed to be dogged by his father, though he felt calmed by Giotto's tower, by Santa Maria del Fiore, by streets he knew from having walked them in states of mounting self-destructive frenzy. He had a longing to talk to some of his companions again, clear up misunderstandings and describe how he'd ruined himself for a reason he couldn't tell: much as he disliked having secrets and now felt a keen need for something he'd got to hide, something that was perhaps his inmost self.

At the approach to the Ponte alle Grazie sat a lemon-seller under a green sunshade with wooden ribs. A few porters and nondescript persons dozed against the embankment wall.

A lark flew from the trees of San Miniato towards the Cascine, like something that sparkled.

Going towards the Piazza della Signoria, cool and sprinkled with water, pedestrians reappeared, increasing to crowds in Via Calzaioli and in the Piazza del Duomo. At the bottom of Via Cavour the Fiesole hill, high and green.

At Badia, when he got off the tram, Pietro blushed

though there was nobody about. He peered under the shutters to see any face there might be scanning the street: nothing but dusty geraniums.

When Ghisola opened the door, but without asking him in, he at once complained she hadn't gone to Radda yet. She replied she'd been waiting for him and wanted first to make sure her parents would have her back.

Inexplicable, the sensation he'd been with her there a long time.

– Why shouldn't they? Are they unkind to you?

– I don't care to stay there.

It struck him as significant she'd answered just that way and not otherwise. He caressed her, pleading:

– You shouldn't deny me, you should be waiting at home. It will give me pleasure.

Then he thought: *Why do I ask her to do that?*

– If you wish . . .

Seeing she was about to comply he asked:

– Come to Siena with me then.

She smiled and signalled to him not to say any more.

He was convinced that giving in to his suggestion must make her feel a great tenderness for him but Ghisola felt more like joking than anything else and asked:

– Don't you like me so much?

– Why shouldn't I like you so much?

He fondled her face all over. She drew back and looked at his fingertips.

– Why won't you let me? I'll wait for you in the street, near the abbey.

– I'll be there. Now go.

He kissed both her hands, holding them together, while she drew away, almost shutting the door in his face.

As he went downstairs he thought: *She's been through a hard time. It's painful for her to live in a strange house. Perhaps her parents have stopped writing, the others are envious. She seemed more sensual but I have to show her just as much respect as before, more even. Otherwise, afterwards, I'd hate her.*

But he didn't think it significant she could leave just like that, as soon as he spoke.

Signor Alberto was involved in bankruptcy proceedings and for the past fortnight had been making himself scarce. She seldom saw him and then only for the odd half-hour in a lawyer's office where he now spent all his time. He'd begged her to go back to Radda just till the proceedings were over, partly so that his in-laws, who were some of his creditors, shouldn't make it any hotter for him.

He had no cash left and several times Ghisola had had to make do with bread helped down with some fruit. Not wanting to go home and not having anywhere else to go she'd been biding her time till she could come to a decision.

So when Pietro turned up all she had to do was tell Beatrice to say goodbye to her lover for her and ask him not to forget her.

All the same she needed further persuasion from Beatrice to remind her Pietro was waiting. Signor Alberto evidently turned to Beatrice for this sort of service too.

The maid embraced her tearfully, with a tenderness that made her smile as she wept.

Waiting at a distance from the door Pietro expected every step he heard would be Ghisola's. At last he saw her.

Neither spoke a word. Between them there was a sort of respectful hostility. Her eyes roved round and his kept following hers, which avoided looking at him yet seemed to see him just the same. But starting with a few remarks they were obliged to exchange the constraint relaxed.

When the tram stopped they got in.

She was wearing a straw hat with a plain black velvet band, a light veil over her face and white cotton gloves.

Pietro noted this plebeian elegance and, moved by it, touched her hand. Once they were married of course he'd have her dress much better. But everybody looked at her and he was glad for her sake.

They hurried to the station from the Piazza del Duomo as the train was leaving soon. The crowd in the streets recalled them to themselves and their purpose, startling them. Then they looked each other in the eye. But they took the Siena train, scarcely speaking. Not till their compartment emptied did he say:

– Why don't you put your veil up?

And he added in a whisper:

– I'll be able to see you better.

She did so, and they sat facing each other.

– If you want to have a rest I'll come and sit beside you. Do you want to lean your head on my shoulder?

– It's all right.

The looks they gave each other seemed to bind them together, so did their leaden souls.

The countryside sped by, too fast! To Pietro it seemed to be running away from him, unwilling to understand him any more, or rather in disapprobation. It increased his need to love Ghisola.

But the daylight was fading, like his excitement. In bright morning sun the carriages had looked ready to burn and burst into flame. Now at every halt they seemed afraid to stay on the new tracks, all interlocking, straight or curved, and glistening with a dull dead light that bore them away into the dim and insubstantial distance. The landscape changed like his states of mind but didn't belong to him.

A train drawing out at Poggibonso gradually shrank till nothing was left of it but the last coach seen end-on, and you couldn't tell if it was stationary or in motion: like some of his illusions. The coaches being shunted up and down, their wheels turning with an unchanging action, one after the other on the same rails, and the goods trucks painted

139

red with figures in white, sealed and patient, brought tears to his eyes. They all jangled his soul, crushed it!

He felt lonely and forsaken and had forgotten all about Ghisola who, sitting opposite, was watching him with intent curiosity. At such times her eyes had a fascinating fixity.

After a sigh he saw them in that state and exclaimed:

– You love me more today!

She gave him a contemptuous stare but to hide it quickly lowered her eyelids, feeling her soul was whisking them off.

Not catching on Pietro waited for her to say something in her turn.

So Ghisola made him sit beside her and they held hands.

The passengers getting in and getting out, the station signals going on and going off, increased her annoyance.

At Siena she refused to go to her aunt's.

– But why not?

– She'll want to know too much. I don't want to tell the others anything.

She was getting her own way, living as she wanted to! He felt she was strong and independent. But to make sure she wasn't doing it to hide something he said:

– It's not right. She's your aunt.

– Suppose I went to a hotel?

– Seeing you on your own they'd have suspicions.

– But you know I'm your girl don't you?

She wheedled using a childish voice, coaxing him, tapping him on the arm with her fan:

– Please. Let me. You always want to have your own way. Tonight you'll let your Ghisola have hers, won't you?

They had to decide because it was only a short walk to the restaurant and getting dark.

Behind the basilica of San Francesco they saw a low-lying bank of clouds like fire.

Someone slowed down to have a better look at them and then they walked faster.

Part of Siena with the church of the Madonna di Provenzano came into view on their left. All the houses looked packed too tight together.

Without noticing each had left off speaking. The Via Vallerozzi looked like a flight of broad roofs going up to the ancient fortress of Salimbeni, its scarp covered by the black shadow of a large spruce fir. Somewhere beyond the fortress was the top of the Tower and, further off, the cupola of the Madonna di Provenzano, almost surrounded by houses at the same level. Whereas the roofs of the three streets meeting at Porta Ovile droop to one side, as if the houses couldn't stand upright. A stretch of one of the streets was like a stony abyss and a woman standing still in it looked trapped.

All the pitched roofs levelled out and the whole row of houses leant on the last, the lowest.

Interrupting his reverie Pietro wagged her hand and resumed their talk:

– You mustn't mind if I'm against it . . . Listen to what I say.

She halted again, impatient.

– Listen . . . I'll tell you what. I'll take you for a meal at my father's. I told him I was going to Poggibonso, a friend of mine lives there. I'll say I met you on the train.

She waited for someone to stop eyeing her and then answered:

– Will he believe us?

– Of course he will!

Ghisola held her head down a long while, not to think it over but to force herself not to think of anything else, and then answered:

– I don't much care for it.

They dropped the subject as they felt close to squabbling. Then, after one of those silences where everything becomes

141

audible, he took her by the arm till they got to the restaurant doorstep.

When Domenico saw them come in he greeted Ghisola but kept away from her and swallowed on the spot the excuse Pietro gave, for Pietro had never told lies.

Rebecca's husband stopped with a plate in his hand and said:

– As soon as I've served these gentlemen I'll go and tell your aunt.

Seeing the aunt could be a pretext for coming to Siena Ghisola thanked him.

Domenico, in good humour, smiled at her: she looked quite different from what she had been at Poggio a' Meli. He went into the kitchen and raising his voice ordered supper for Pietro and her, like he did for customers but adding bluntly:

– Those don't pay!

Ghisola gave an easy laugh. Only pride made her dislike being treated by Domenico for what she was, but Pietro made her mad. He wasn't a bit sharp and he counted for nothing in his own home!

To show she didn't need to eat in the restaurant she wouldn't sit at a table but Pietro begged her under his breath not to be awkward and said things would be cleared up next day.

Domenico had been shuttling between the kitchen and the room they were in, his hands in his pockets and his head down, never looking at them. He went out to blow off steam with his friend the chemist: it was all very well for a son to go gallivanting while he was young but he shouldn't bring his girls home! But the chemist made fun of his indignation and told him to let the lad enjoy himself, the girl was a good-looker.

Ghisola didn't lift her head while eating and hardly seemed to have any appetite. Gently Pietro pressed his foot against hers and made a remark or two to dispel her moodiness. Then he left her in the restaurant to have a word with her cousin Rosaura, beside the pantry, where it was not so light. And accompanied by her, Ghisola crossed the street to see her aunt, telling her a tissue of clever inventions with the most ingenuous air. Rebecca said:

– I've got nowhere for you to sleep tonight. You can sleep with your cousin if the master agrees.

Ghisola came down again and re-entered the restaurant, curious to see how she'd end up!

It was nearly midnight and the tables had been cleared. The cooks drowsed against the trencher block. The ovens were going out, as if the embers were falling asleep too. All the lamps were turned down low and the restaurant reeked of the repulsive stench of food from various dishes mixed up.

In a skep by the sink, peelings and leavings.

Unexpectedly it got darker and for a few minutes it rained: one of the rains that bring out bad temper, like those that reactivate muck-heaps in the fields.

Tired and sleepy Ghisola felt it raining in her heart yet not washing it out. She felt just as stifled.

Occasionally summer lightning flashed between clouds.

She had an idea she'd felt that rain before, in a dream, but avoided thinking about it so as not to miss what was happening round her and what people were saying to her.

Domenico, waking up from the sofa where he'd got into the habit of snoozing at least a couple of hours before he went to bed, issued the order:

– Lock up.

He was so plainly put out Rebecca only spoke to him because she had to:

– I'm going across to the house to get sheets for Ghisola.

Domenico said nothing either way and turned aside when Ghisola, passing close by him, wished him good-night in a manner almost provocative.

The ceiling of Rosaura's bedroom was so low, lying on one of the beds she could touch a rafter. A window-slit in a wall a metre thick looked into a narrow courtyard dank even in summer.

When the bed was made up Ghisola took her jacket off and asked:

– Where does Pietro sleep?

– In the room he had when he was little. Like to go and see him? What big arms you've got!

– Feel how fat I am!

She made her pinch her side and then left.

Remembering the house she half-groped her way across the hall and then through the parlour, not so dark there because of the light from the electric street-lamps.

The door to Pietro's room was open, as Domenico had to pass through it to reach his own. She saw the desk with books on it, the tallboy with the shimmering looking-glass. She went further in, to the bed set against the wall: Pietro was asleep.

She bent over and started kissing him on the mouth. Without quite waking up he felt a thrill and called out loud:

– It's you, Ghisola!

Pietro couldn't make out why Ghisola harboured grudges against her family. As far as he could see they were just whims. He complained to Rebecca, advising her to have a word with her niece. He added:

– She must learn to read at least. She's promised me she would.

But Ghisola knew how to get something put out of mind by bringing up something else.

He supposed she'd taken offence, at Domenico and the restaurant and all that, and was only looking for an excuse to flounce out. The very morning after their arrival she'd said:

– And do you think I'd stay with your father even if he wants me here?

Pietro didn't feel he could promise her anything. He said:

– When he's as sure as I am the stories are all untrue then he'll respect you. Why shouldn't he? Why shouldn't he respect you, why shouldn't he accept you as my wife?

He held her by the arm but knowing it was more hopeless than ever she said:

– He hates me. And he doesn't want us to love each other. Don't you remember he sent me away from Poggio a' Meli because we loved each other even then?

All his plans became as ridiculous to him as once they had seemed serious, each one more than the others, and Pietro agreed he should let her go where she wanted. He felt remorse for having her sent to Radda! He didn't even dare keep hold of her arm.

Knowing she couldn't be staying more than a day or two Ghisola took nothing to heart and at once let Domenico know she was off. With Pietro as escort she went to Poggio a' Meli, staying with her grandparents, so never set foot in the restaurant again.

The olive-trees were dressed in a fine white tissue illuminated by fireflies while on the black Chianti hills lightning came and went like thick liquid light.

Ghisola was sitting by herself on the dwarf wall of the threshing-floor. Masa and the other labourers' wives, in the moonlight, increased her petulance. She fancied the moonlight was hanging onto their clothes and trailing round after them as they moved about. Far away, they didn't even remember she was still alive: filthy sluts, like she had been!

She stretched herself out on top of the wall, giving a convulsive shudder, and stared at one star bigger than the rest. It seemed to be going round and round and then to skip about here and there: she felt her temples throb in time with its motion.

Thinking she was going out of her mind she tossed her head sharply and rubbed her eyes.

The women went back in and she sat up and looked towards the doors. Nearly half the yard was in shadow, as far as the well and an archway where a waggon stood, but to her these only appeared to be other shadows different in colour.

It was the same dwarf wall as where she and some play-mates had sat all day long, swatting flies on their knees. What laughs they'd had whenever anyone went by on the road!

The well frightened her, as though it was dragging her and the moon down into the water. Then thinking the moonlight was shining on her face as well she hid it in her hands and stayed like that.

Soon she heard somebody padding across the threshing-floor towards her, obviously barefoot. She didn't move, imagining she couldn't, though she knew it wasn't true. Then Carlo sat down beside her. First he coughed and after another moment laid a hand on her breast.

She lifted her face without looking at him, gave a laugh and went indoors.

Carlo had the impression he'd seen the laugh, not the girl.

Pietro reached the open farm-gate soon after. Before calling in at Giacco's he stopped to gaze at the moon, it looked as if it had just sailed out of the back windows.

He thought the labourers would admire his love for a country girl, one of themselves.

Ghisola and he went to the fields by the path that ran from the threshing-floor to the cherry-tree where they'd talked many years before. The memory seemed still there, under the branches.

Ghisola was jumpy and ready to give herself. She nearly said: *Why can't you see?* But Pietro was in increasing ecstasy. To him it was almost like dream-walking. He said:

– Why don't you look at me?

She did in fact only make cursory turns of the head in his direction and would have liked to leave him there. But controlling herself, as she did when she lay on her back on top of the wall and counterfeiting his tone of voice, she stopped to look up at the sky. Duped he cried out:

– We'll never have another night like this! The stars are shining in your eyes too! I can see them!

He gave her a long kiss. She tossed her head and moved away. Was he mad? He made her stop again, shouting with excitement. Beside herself with sex Ghisola was like a jug that finally comes apart along a hairline crack. She couldn't help saying:

– If you were a man!

He answered as though speaking to himself:

– I love you!

And as his ecstasy too was becoming sexual he turned to go back: Ghisola mustn't even notice!

Masa was waiting at the top of the path, arms akimbo. She was disturbed by the suggestive banter of the labourers sitting round the threshing-floor. Giacco had crept back indoors, annoyed he had to keep the oil-lamp on. A moth with a body as thick as a finger thudded against it. The whirr of its wings every so often aflutter made him lift his head and peep through the crack of the door.

Pietro and Ghisola slackened their embrace as they skirted the threshing-floor, while Masa whispered:

– Don't go too far.

The labourers went quiet, partly out of consideration for the young master, and in the moonlight their faces looked unlined.

The staddle of the straw-stack had been left leaning against a lime-tree.

Fun at Poggio a' Meli!

Outside the gate they held hands again.

The fireflies swarming among the pale olive leaves seemed to be increasing in number all the time. Some stuck to their hands as if they were gummed.

They began to kiss, she supporting herself on the timber paling, he pressing himself against her, both being hidden in the shadow of the hedge. All at once Pietro noticed she was making randy full-hipped movements. He stepped back and reproved her.

Masa was losing patience and after standing awhile on the threshing-floor, stopping her mouth to prevent herself answering the labourers she couldn't help listening to, called out just then and Pietro and Ghisola went in.

A few of the labourers, overcome with hilarity, scratched their heads hard. Bending forward with his palms over his knees Carlo jeered at Masa whenever he glanced at her. In one hand he felt he was holding what he had touched.

The talk about them went on for over a month.

Carlo would stand for a while spying on them from his door when they came his way, he felt he simply couldn't go to bed without saying something to Ghisola.

But Ghisola asked one of the labourers' daughters to come with her when she saw Pietro back to town, so as not to have to walk home by herself.

They walked arm-in-arm while the other girl, not daring to come too close, kept at a distance. But turning round they saw her smiling, watchful and agitated, then almost convulsively.

Before parting they gave each other more kisses. Then the girl, who had covered her face with her hands, peeping at them through her fingers, dropped down in the middle of the roadway and rolled in the dust. She cried out, as though she'd been alone:

– Oh oh, what am I doing!

– Put something on.

Finding her in her bedroom with arms bare he wanted her to slip her pink jacket on. He waited before kissing her and then said:

– I like you better like this. Otherwise I couldn't kiss you. You know.

She was to leave by the Radda coach.

Things were unchanged. Domenico had pretended to ignore Pietro and Ghisola, knowing how to hold himself in check and being sure time was on his side. And the sly talk hadn't been proved wrong: Pietro hadn't found a way to advance the wedding.

Masa was in and out, darting one glance at them and one at the yard, to see if the labourers were there, prying or eavesdropping. More than ever she dreaded the clack of their tongues and out of regard for the master looked forward to Ghisola's departure.

She didn't feel it befitted her, that her granddaughter should become Pietro's wife, it was something that surpassed her aspirations. She didn't dare thank God for it either, she was afraid she'd be punished for self-satisfaction. Besides she wanted to be sure first! On other occasions she'd said:

– We can't ask God for something we're not worthy to have.

Pietro handed Ghisola her comb and did up her jacket at the back. The last button done, she turned round and got herself another kiss.

As there was still plenty of time she lay down on the bed where she'd slept as a young girl. Her face hardened till it took on a look of severe pain. She repulsed all Pietro's caresses, refused to be kissed and didn't even answer him, whatever he tried to say. She frowned, with clouded eyes and pouting mouth.

Masa asked:

– Are you ill? What's the matter?

Ghisola drew her head back as though her neck had gone stiff. Pietro took her hands in his:

– It's nothing. It'll pass. But where do you feel the pain? Let her be, Masa.

Ghisola looked at them both, first him, then her. Pietro kissed her feet and she hid them under her skirt. Was it dislike of going away? But it was similar to times he'd pacified himself by touching one of her belongings: a ribbon, a brooch or her silver bangle. And he couldn't admit she might have exchanged one of her trinkets with somebody else!

Ghisola would have liked not to move again. She thought she'd have to stay like that indefinitely, perhaps for ever.

Pietro and Masa fussing about her gave her the shivers. She could have kicked them.

When Pietro persuaded her to get up, saying otherwise they'd miss the coach, she had a return of the longing to say something affectionate and her mouth made a wry yet graceful grimace.

She grew calmer as they came nearer the place where the coach was to pass. She walked with knees bent, letting her parasol knock against one of them at every step. Leaning her weight on Masa and Pietro she took on the appearance of a child.

Masa was still thinking about the labourers and the house left open. She turned about, twisting her lips.

The coach was late. So Masa went, clasping her hands over her abdomen and saying:

– Let's make sure it all turns out for the best!

Ghisola didn't even say goodbye and separated herself from Pietro, who never stopped looking at her.

There was no one at the windows of the Palazzo dei Diavoli. On the way they'd seen a farmer's threshing-floor heaped with corn-stooks. The sunlight had seemed to pour down from the farmhouse roof and rebound from the ground in a ring of flame.

From where they'd stopped they could see, on the top of a high hill, Vico Bello in its walled orchard. The whole hill was green with maize, while the olive-trees looked colourless and transparent. Vine-rows thickened by their own shadows.

A beggar sat down on the steps of the Capella, in whose shade they were standing too. They pointed him out to each other, smiling at having had the same thought and waiting to see him eat the bread he clutched in both hands.

The coach arrived. Inside were a woman and a country-man with a gaunt unshaven face: a patient fetched from hospital by his wife. Beside him he held some medicines tied up in a red handkerchief, over her knees she had a grey shawl she'd put round him at nightfall. The man's eyes were dimmed and he seemed restless, as though he hadn't wanted the coach to stop, expecting something to disturb him.

Drawn down to keep the sun out, the blinds undulated.

The horse had pulled up sharp, lowering its haunches. It was lean and scraggy, one of those high-headed animals with big jaws. In harness brilliant with brasses its ribs expanded as it breathed. An oat straw had caught under the bit between its wrinkled lips. It leant for support against the shafts. It stank of sweat.

151

Pietro opened the coach-door painted with the postal arms. Ghisola climbed in, holding her head down. She indicated she wanted to be kissed and Pietro kissed her but had rather have said: *Not here!* She smiled to herself, at him, while the coach moved off.

After a glance at the couple sitting opposite, as if she hadn't noticed them before, she lowered her head again and paled. She had felt a pregnancy pang.

In almost deathly anguish Pietro waited in vain to see her turn round.

It was getting on for September when he went to see her at Radda.

This village, a collection of houses you keep in view some kilometres before you reach it through a tract of scrubland, on the brow of a rise, is so quiet, from the road you can hear people talking indoors.

Pietro had ridden as far as La Castellina in the motorcar of an acquaintance who was to wait for him there in the evening to take him back to Siena.

From there to Radda he walked from one end of the scrub to the other, threading his way round boulders and in between juniper-bushes and oak-trees, from time to time catching a whiff of the smell left by a flock of sheep.

At the side of the old disused road he saw a blue-painted niche in a wall behind three slim cypresses with gnarled boles. The wall began at the niche but had collapsed a few metres further on. On top of the rubble was ivy together with a big hawthorn.

Round about were other hill-top copses, denser and closer together the further away they were, in colour fading to a thin wash.

He came to Poggiarofani, a halt for shepherds who pass that way. There the road is at its highest and all twists and turns, switchbacking between the Aretine Apennines and the Monte di Santa Fiora, but these are so far away, they look like sky, like the horizon.

Birds flushed from the valleys either side brushed past him and then, as if not knowing where to fly next, after making a tack disappeared down into the depths again.

When he reached the village, tired and out of temper, his feeling of elation wavered and the facts against him presented themselves to his mind. He knew his father would insult him and nearly everyone would think he came to Ghisola for sex.

Passing the first houses he let go by a carriage whited with dust.

He inquired about Ghisola from a woman who'd been keeping him under observation since she caught sight of him, while her jug under a water-spout brimmed over. He was told she was staying with her married elder sister, Lucia. He had the door pointed out to him and finding it open went in but came out again to knock.

Three other women had already gathered in the lane, curious to know who he was, and to avoid their stares he went up the steps without waiting for an answer.

Lucia, who'd met him once at Poggio a' Meli, came towards him at the top of the steps. Without a word of greeting he asked:

– Where's Ghisola?

If Lucia hadn't been her sister he'd have been angry with her for not telling him without being asked, as if she didn't know how he loved her.

Seeing his urgency Lucia answered:

– Upstairs.

Irritably he said:

– Call her . . . No, I'll call her.

But hearing him Ghisola appeared of her own accord.

153

In a few days she had browned. She was in a torn skirt that reached the floor.

As the two of them were standing looking at each other without speaking Lucia went back into the kitchen to prepare the meal.

– Why aren't you staying with your parents?

Still she looked at him without answering. Then with sincere wonderment she asked:

– Do you still love me?

The question disturbed him and he said:

– Why do you ask? Why shouldn't I love you?

He made a move to twist her wrist. Her eyes fixed on the ground, she let him, not caring.

– You oughtn't to be dressed like this . . . Suppose somebody should see you?

He repeated, to know how she would answer:

– Suppose somebody should see you?

Ghisola kept silent, apparently hurt, and Pietro was sorry, like when you strike an animal and then realize there was no reason to.

– You're showing your legs . . . Your skirt's undone.

The words he hadn't meant to say made his eyes prickle. To avoid being tempted he took her arm and pushed her into her room. Ghisola stepped back to make him let go and with that the dress split all the way up and he saw her hip. She blushed. He hid her face in an embrace so that she shouldn't be ashamed!

– I saw . . . but I didn't mean to.

She gathered the torn seam to, though ready to take her dress right off, and said:

– Let me go.

– Why do you wear it then?

Pietro asked, regretting he'd caressed her at that moment.

– I've only myself to please. What have you come to Radda for? Just for me? There are other girls! Have you got it in for me as well?

– There are some things you mustn't talk to me about today!

– There's always something I mustn't talk about according to you!

– Perhaps it's not true? Have I ever told you off without reason?

There was a lump in his throat and he wanted to leave off.

– But if you don't like me in this, why . . .?

– Because I love you don't I?

Then she broke into a lewd laugh. He went on, with drying lips:

– Perhaps you wouldn't mind if I didn't love you?

And surprised by her silence he added:

– I forgive you. Give me a kiss.

She turned towards him with a slow shy movement, as though afraid to concede too much. When they were about to kiss she drew back. Pietro lifted her bent head, firmly and forcibly, saying:

– Don't cry.

He was afraid of seeing that inward quivering of the lips that seems to bring up tears from a source a long way down. Still holding her head in his hands he said more submissively, almost pleading, in desperation:

– Listen.

She looked at him.

– Perhaps you don't want to marry me?

She kept looking at him and then, in the way that worked so well on him, made as if to choke back tears. And because she didn't cry he thought her touchingly kind.

Bending down he covered her throat with kisses. Then he made her look at him so that they fixed each other in the eye.

– Why should you need to be unfaithful to me?

He uttered the expression with his throat strangled with repugnance, with the whole of his moral loathing.

155

Detecting the suspicion she kept silent.

Pietro again took her face in his hands, that face as hard as flint, turning it so that she had to look at him. She twisted like a lizard when it turns tail and darts off.

– You thought you'd stay out of my sight for good?

She told him he'd guessed right, unloosed her hands from his and turned her back on him.

He studied her in that position a long time, at a loss what to do.

But afraid he might do something to get even with her she yielded and gave him a smile. He embraced and kissed her. She said:

– But it's not me you're in love with.

He didn't understand and took her up sharply:

– Why do you always say things like that?

He came out in a cold sweat but tried to control himself, caressing her and saying:

– So I'm not in love with you?

Then she said, calmly and without any feeling:

– You'll marry someone else.

He went pale but had the strength to take a few steps towards the door. Ghisola cried out, with the intention of hurting him:

– Do you love me like this?

First she offered him her mouth. He hesitated, then let the intoxicating sensation pour through him.

Wanting to give herself to him, so he'd think that was how she'd got pregnant, Ghisola asked:

– Why did you touch me just now?

Pietro wouldn't tell her. But Ghisola exclaimed:

– I know why. I've guessed. You're touching me differently now. You want me too. You can't help it. Anyway if you want me, I'm yours.

But Lucia called from the kitchen and the three of them had lunch together: the sister's husband was away.

At two it was time for Pietro to think of going back and he told Ghisola. She'd forgotten and cried out gaily:

– Stay the night.

– My father's expecting me. You know he'd turn nastier, against you as well.

Ghisola persisted:

– Sleep here. I'll come and give you a kiss like that time in Siena.

He was afraid they might sleep together and refused. Guessing, Ghisola said:

– Aren't we together in the daytime and don't do anything wrong?

And with a guileless air she added:

– I swear you'll respect me, because you won't . . .

– No. You must be my wife first. And I say it because I love you.

Her body soaked with sex like a sponge with oil she went into another room, shutting the door behind her. She reappeared almost immediately, while he was wondering whether to wait for her to go away. In an almost tearful voice imitating hers he said:

– We'll be together later on. Now we deny ourselves. We have to.

Holding her by the waist he shook her.

– Answer me.

Ghisola hid her face in her apron, simulating an innocence so natural it would have taken anybody in.

– Why are you hiding your face? Don't. I won't have it.

They went downstairs with their hands interlocked and as she had a timid and bashful look he felt sorry for her. He couldn't believe it possible he'd been capable of scolding her.

At the bottom of the steps Ghisola leant against the doorsill. He stood with one foot on the roadway and waited for her to say something but, as she didn't seem even to be thinking of him any more, said nothing else to her and slowly made his way out of the village. Several times he'd have liked to look back.

Ghisola shook herself and stared at the place where he'd

157

been standing. Her hands placed together on the corner of the sill she thrust her trunk forward till she stood free. Then she went back indoors.

To her sister she didn't say anything about Pietro.

For Ghisola, Pietro's love had been a reawakening of conscience. She felt she had to deceive him to prevent herself being humiliated by him. The stronger and wilder his love for her the more she found it necessary to defend herself, not because she wanted him or wanted to rehabilitate herself but to stop him finding everything out. She wanted to have the upper hand, get herself accepted for what she was and so be able to feel he was implicated in the blame she'd brought on herself.

If after her baby was born she managed to get him to marry her she was sure she'd have absolute sway over his character, twist him round her little finger!

Basically she thought herself better and more attractive than when she'd been a silly ill-dressed country girl. Cleverer too, sharper, and pride didn't allow her to recognize the painful disillusion Pietro would have.

She only wanted to take advantage of him because he was well enough off to save her from her condition of permanent insecurity. She was frightened of growing old before she found true affection. So hostility to Pietro's demand she should keep herself pure for him turned into something like hatred when she was afraid of being found out.

His naïvety was another serious obstacle, not a weakness she could smile at coolly. Day by day she felt she was losing ground, for Pietro was always the same, quick to wound her with his heedless adoration.

She thought him selfish: rightly from one point of view, for if anything should leak out he'd never forgive her. So she couldn't accept his way of loving her but never thought of changing her way of life, to indemnify herself for the continual humiliation, till she was obliged to. All she felt was a sort of remorse and this made Pietro sympathetic to her.

But it's true it never occurred to her she ought to have been frank with him right from the start, so that he could understand.

On the contrary she considered she hadn't deceived him to the point of making him believe she was pregnant by him!

Also she wanted to get her own back on Domenico. It was a malignant pleasure to make his son lose his head over her.

Besides, what Pietro demanded seemed to her ridiculous: soppy nonsense, not right for a fellow.

What was he after? Why was he in love with her and not with some young lady of Siena out of his own station in life?

True, she plumed herself on it for her grandparents' and all her family's sake. She might become a signora and lead a life of leisure, so they had to look up to her. And then she'd done nothing to pleasure Pietro, not that way, nothing for him to remember her by, so Domenico had better shut up. It was his son who was taking unfair advantage of her, she'd been a servant of theirs. It was she who had to trust him!

At the same time she had many memories of her stay at Poggio a' Meli. She'd become attached to the place and when she went back enjoyed hearing the compliments paid her by the labourers' wives. Somewhat ambiguous ones, it's true, implying they didn't have Pietro's trustfulness or Giacco's and Masa's. leniency.

At Radda her parents hadn't dared say anything because the first evening she came in she said she'd go straight back

159

and they weren't to take any notice of the gossip they heard about her because it wasn't true anyhow.

Actually her parents took credit that she dressed even better than the daughter of the mayor, who had pots of money. Her sisters envied her, each saying to herself she was artfuller than they were. And being fond of her the family were the first to speak up in her defence.

Borio had died of pneumonia, his rival the farm-manager had aged prematurely and the two or three times he met Ghisola called her Miss, going red in the face and raising his hat.

In the village she wasn't judged too harshly and anyway the rumour soon got about she was going to marry the son of the owner of *The Blue Fish*.

Everybody recalled her past but laughed without malice, even reckoning she'd always been a good girl, barring one or two scandals. Besides it was to show respect for her parents, who were rather poor.

But after being let down by her lover at Badia a Ripoli Ghisola had begun to feel somewhat anxious.

Those months at Badia a Ripoli often came back to her. There she'd enjoyed being free and independent, and with the certainty signor Alberto was coming home every evening.

True it had meant staying outside Florence, rather in the country, but she'd never wanted for anything. She could go to Florence whenever she liked so long as somebody went with her.

She had the bedroom overlooking the garden that had given Pietro a scare and the dining-room in the front, with no houses opposite.

Instead there was only a wall lower than corn in the ear and a cypress that in summer got smothered in bindweed. On the wall, filled in and topped with nothing but mortar, primroses rooted and the sort of grass that has yellow flowers.

Further off was a clear sparkling brook where clothes

were washed and then spread out on the green beside a gate with two square pillars, two terracotta dogs on top, glaring at each other.

The corn made a dust and the washing laid out to dry flew about like the kites boys brought from the Campo di Marte.

She could lean over the kitchen balcony to call the woman who sold fruit and from there order what she wanted from the baskets set out below. A little further along was a cooked-meat shop that sold cheese and wine as well and when the wind was in that art you smelt all its aromas. Nearby lived families of well-to-do employees and a few market-gardeners. And as she kept herself to herself nobody thought of being shocked.

Now she had to earn her living day by day. But the lower she sank and the more she rotted in that way of life, the more she grew to value Pietro, precisely because she felt totally unable to be what he wanted her to be, even for one hour. Because of that it came to matter less to her and she stopped feeling the moral disquiet that had troubled her in the first months.

That's how it was with her and every day she became more resigned to it. Besides it was no use leaving off.

Pietro's letters left her with the impression he took her for an innocent tender-hearted bride-to-be. Smiling she pitied him.

In September he went back to Florence, ostensibly for the resit exams. He grumbled at the waste of time but thought it right, a sort of penalty, to stay away from his books and his fellow-students, who cut him dead. It was like going into hiding, putting himself in the wrong with everyone.

161

But this wilful plunge into the depths, provoked by his anguish, made his heart swell: it beat for something else!

Now he never left his digs in Via Cimabue except to eat. That he couldn't help, though sorry to do it and tempted to abstain.

Ghisola, already in Florence before he arrived, was staying in one of those so-called private houses, where she earned very good money. Learning of his arrival from a letter of Pietro's forwarded from Radda she at once went to see him, if only to allay any suspicion.

When the landlady, who'd let her in, made a move to call him she signalled her to stay where she was and walking without making a noise tapped with her fingertips on the door of his room. Guessing who it was he jumped to his feet and opened it.

Ghisola pretended she didn't want to come in. He drew her inside and kissed her, trembling all over. Smiling and warding him off she said:

– That's enough!

She sat down, first removing her hat and afterwards placing it on her knees. His heart gave a hot jump and he felt his face redden because he couldn't help asking:

– Why did you leave Radda without letting me know?

Her lovely face took on at times a perfect purity and she answered without caring what she was saying:

– I've only just got here. My mistress at Badia a Ripoli insisted I should come back. And at Radda there wasn't anybody I could dictate a letter to, because I didn't want to let on we'd be meeting. Haven't I done right?

– Quite right. She's taking you on again then?

– Yes.

– I'm glad. But I don't suppose you can spend the rest of the day with me?

– I asked her for the day off.

Believing her he embraced her in a rush of gratitude.

They went out at once and strolled round Florence. They had a meal and then talked for a time on one of those seats in the little public garden on Piazza San Marco where they sell spice-cakes and pumpkin-seeds to soldiers and the leisured classes.

When dusk began to fall she said with a laugh:

– I've got to go, if I'm late I won't be let off another time.

They parted. He didn't even trouble to take note which way she went.

Three days he waited for her, indoors all the time, thinking he'd confide in her about the exams, not knowing whether it mattered to her or not. The plan gave him an almost sexual pleasure.

Noises even faint ones he couldn't stand, finding relief in dozing on the bed. It was then his temples seemed to pulse with less stress and his heart swell without him feeling the swelling. But his cold hands gave him a sensation of pain and fear, reminding him of his life in Siena.

If he hadn't been afraid of distressing her he'd have asked Ghisola, with all the tenderness the idea filled him with, to join him in a suicide pact.

But when Ghisola came to see him everything altered. She'd treat him like a lunatic, laughing in his face with that laugh of hers that terrified him, though it made her look more lovely.

They spent another whole day together, like the other time, then not again.

In Siena Pietro made out the exams had gone badly.

More and more he felt he was a victim of the injustices all should rise up together against.

Domenico roared at him:

– What have you been up to? If only you'd worked . . . Aren't you convinced you're not cut out for study?

Pietro thought the outburst deserved but was satisfied Domenico hadn't made any allusion to Ghisola.

His moodiness and anxiety returned, worse now because his love for Ghisola was increasing all the time. Nothing else left any trace, as though nothing else concerned him.

He felt he'd fallen into a void he'd never get out of. Could he blame Ghisola? No: only himself. It was himself he considered lost rather than her. But every morning when he woke up he thought: *If it wasn't for Ghisola I'd kill myself.* All the calm of mind he'd been making his way towards he now saw recede.

Domenico didn't immediately betray his impatience to see Pietro take to the business. But their talks took on the feigned affability that conceals outbursts of anger, so they avoided speaking to each other. Everybody sided with Domenico and expected a bust-up. Pietro understood but pretended not to notice what his father was thinking when he shot him a passing glance.

Sometimes Domenico thought of himself as a plain rough man confronted by a subtle villain. Then he was afraid of coming off worst.

What use had they been, the prolonged efforts he'd filled his life with? At his death wouldn't all he'd amassed by cunning and hard work pass to his son? And it was his son who didn't appreciate it? His son who wanted to pull down all he'd built up!

Then he realized his mistake, allowing him too much rein with Ghisola. He'd received her into the house himself! Now the minx was setting his son against him, teaching him to hate him!

It seemed to him a deliberate betrayal: seminary, art

school, technical school, college, private tutors, the lot!

He'd had those ideas so often, he thought it not the time to give way to them now.

Sitting on the chair he'd used for over twenty years, his hands in his trouser-pockets and his now bald head leaning against the wall, he followed Pietro with his eyes as he moved about. But he didn't say anything, trying to take his mind off it by talking to employees or the odd customer who came to pass the time of day.

Pietro thought of all the household things he'd like to have for himself and Ghisola.

He thought of the oil-lamp, so quiet and always steady, with its tin cap. He thought of his mother's easy-chair: under the padded seat was a sort of wooden box where she kept balls of different-coloured wools and the only books she had, two novels in parts, illustrated. He thought of the four cushions she leant on, each pressed out of shape in its own recognizable way. He thought of the odour of eau de Cologne, the bottles of anthysteric medicine, a small worn gold cross.

Before going to sleep in his hard bed he recalled all the familiar things he had an intense though unconscious affection for. He felt he had to give them a different impress, a different meaning. Ghisola would be the one to make everything new. He had the same sensation of sweetness he had when beside her.

When the candle went out he turned to the wall and slept.

About midnight Domenico passed through the bedroom carrying the brass lamp. Pietro woke up and had an impulse to raise his head. But the other door shut again and he was left with the sense of grievance you have when a frame of mind is broken into.

In the morning Domenico went out very early, not saying anything to Pietro, who was trying to remodulate the dreams we have between sleep and waking, when we seem able to stop sleeping or continue.

165

He sat at his desk, doing nothing, his knees wedged under the drawer. He couldn't believe it possible that everything should lose interest for him, while sensual memories excited him to excess.

He became emotional over his fate to do nothing but suffer: *Why can't I see Ghisola? Nobody else is obliged to give everything up. And nobody troubles about it. I can't understand why others have something to do that I'll never have: the coachman touches his horse up to make it go faster, the sweepers sprinkle the streets.*

He avoided going to the restaurant till lunch-time. Then he had to wait for the right moment so the cook shouldn't answer him back, put up with what they gave him and fetch bread and knife and fork from the pantry himself.

Having loved others ideally he now had a bitter struggle. But his father might say to him:

– Don't stand in the way when the waiters are coming through. You're not working!

He left the restaurant in case his father should try and give him a job to do. *Could I be made to go on an errand to the grocer's to buy cheese? Or take a basket and get it filled with bread? Or argue with somebody who wants a discount? Besides, Ghisola would never marry me then.*

One day he received a letter. The handwriting on the envelope at once gave him a sense something inevitable was going to happen. He was reluctant to open it. He read: *Ghisola is unfaithful to you. If you want proof go to the Via della Pergola.*

There was the number of the house and a woman's name, perhaps false.

The words seemed the answer to a puzzle. He thought: *There must be a real reason.*

All the painful setbacks he'd had recurred to his mind one after the other and he marvelled that a stranger should have had compassion on him.

He cast about for a way to obtain money and take Ghisola by surprise. Rebecca wouldn't lend him any, objecting he hadn't repaid what he'd borrowed before,

But Pietro insisted:

– How can you expect me to ask my father?

– Ask one of your friends.

While speaking she went to the chest of drawers, having made up her mind to lend him the money so that he could establish her niece's innocence. But first she took out a clean nappy for the baby she had in her arms. She spread the nappy on the bed and threw the soiled one under the wardrobe. The baby crying seemed to make her forget about the money.

She still held her head down, as though thinking: If it would do any good she'd go to Domenico on his behalf but this was no matter to get mixed up in. She said:

– You simply must go tomorrow morning?

He answered:

– How can I not after I've had this letter?

She understood and sighed. He waited a little and then said:

– Let me have it.

– How much do you need?

– More than last time.

– Heavens above, how can I afford it? Why don't you put a bit aside each week?

He grieved he'd never thought of it: it seemed impossible to explain.

– I'll save from now on. But this time . . . you let me have it.

If he'd had to wait any longer he wouldn't have had the courage to insist but Rebecca believed his promise and gave in.

Pietro counted the money himself while she leant against the open drawer and probed his face. He smiled and thanked her.

Rebecca saw him to the stairhead, still pleading:

– Don't forget you've got to pay me back.

It was true Ghisola had her letters addressed to Badia a

Ripoli but mightn't she have moved just a few days before? What could it be?

He made an attempt to identify the various possibilities but as he took none of them seriously found it impossible to accept any of them. All his afflictions seemed for the first time distant from him and possible to abolish. His sufferings seemed external and he had a small happiness quite unlike any other. It crossed his mind: *Why did I believe the letter at once?*

During the journey he seemed to be in a state of unconsciousness with fever. But he was in a hurry to arrive.

The train ran alongside the Arno, its water glittering like a million broken mirrors. It passed steep bristling pineries, still dotted with violet shadows, between aspens and silver-leaf poplars, behind telegraph poles: cypresses clumped, as if set apart from other cypresses. It made its approach to the city, over where a soft blue was gathering, between hills each smoother than the one before. The wonder of that beauty made him humble. While the love he'd had for Ghisola came to seem an abominable indignity, he couldn't say why: *Could it be I don't love her?*

He went in at the door indicated by the letter, making his way through a knot of women who didn't stand aside. The staircase, dark and dirty, smelt of body-odours and face-powder.

On the first floor, through a door left ajar, he caught sight of a prostitute in a pink dressing-gown. She threw him a sardonic glance.

On the second floor was another flat-door also half-open. He stopped to listen. He heard a few women chattering cheerfully, one humming. He thought of the worst explanation and then of the best. But he shuddered: *Can Ghisola be one of those?* And he climbed the next stairs faster, as though to escape.

He halted on the top floor, out of breath. There was a sitting-room with an oval table in the centre. His vision blurred. Then he made out a woman lying on a sofa in conversation with a soldier whose beret was some way away on a chair.

The woman took fright at Pietro: he was staring in consternation at her. She touched the soldier's knee and both turned their eyes on him. He took another step forward but seemed to have no legs. It was like a nightmare he refused to believe real. He babbled something but the woman didn't answer. He thought he'd offended her and was about to go. But at that moment Ghisola came in through an open door. Seeing him she stopped short and paled, almost fainted, but then turned back, supporting herself with an elbow along the wall, like a mouse that turns round when it's half-crushed by a blow.

In order not to yield to a sensation he was losing his balance after being gripped by some force, Pietro followed her blindly into a room where all he saw was the window.

She'd already taken off her dirty jacket when he came in but had had to sit down to disguise her maternity bump.

He bent down to kiss her, tears in his eyes:

– Why are you like this?

She didn't know how to answer. *Has he seen I'm pregnant? When shall I tell him? I knew this would happen.* Then she spoke:

– There are only women here.

Instantly he disbelieved her and answered:

– I'm not having it. Get dressed. How did you get that bruise on your arm?

She was afraid she'd trip herself up but answered:

– I bit myself.

169

He thought it might be true. Then after a pause, in which he hoped everything would clear up, he said:

– Let's get out of here, I want to talk.

– Let's stay. I'm not going out today.

There was another pause that made him think: *Why don't I ask her what way she's unfaithful to me? I'll never find anything out like this. What can I say?*

– I don't like this house. What sort of house is it?

– I'll tell you. It isn't anything bad.

Several times she'd thought of confessing the pregnancy but it looked impossible now and she tried to hide it so as not to be caught off guard. He decided to speak sharper:

– Stand up.

The madam came in, a strongly-built broad-shouldered woman wearing round her waist a belt of white leather: a midwife who boarded expectant mothers.

Pietro turned towards her, daunted by the effect his suspicions might produce. He tried to explain why he was there. The woman knew all about it and saw no help for Ghisola. She was afraid he'd kill her.

Ghisola was looking at the window ready to throw herself out in an hysterical seizure pregnancy might bring on.

The woman lingered, tidying the wash-stand, refolding a hand-towel, keeping Pietro under watch out of the corner of her eye and trying to ask Ghisola what she should do.

Pietro waited for her to go. Her fidgeting was getting on his nerves. Finally, with a great effort, he said:

– I want to be alone with Ghisola.

Meanwhile Ghisola had slipped another blouse on, without rising from the sofa and without him seeing anything, and she said to the woman:

– Go then . . . Leave it to me.

But she was as terrified as ever and felt any moment she'd sink to her knees.

The woman went out warily, not closing the door and positioning herself to listen. Pietro noticed and, before

170

asking Ghisola to explain anything, made to fasten it but had difficulty working the catch. Not that he wanted to hurt her, with the questions he had to ask, he was more inclined to put them off.

She stood up:

– Don't shut it . . . Nobody can hear us.

Then, turning to her with a look full of devotion and affection, he saw her belly.